With his life in tatters, Vietnam veteran Richard hits the road hoping to find work where he can forget his past and leave his demons behind. He finds work on a rundown farm owned by a woman with two children whose husband is away at the war.

Rebecca struggles with everyday life, including an overbearing father-in-law, a retired army officer, the Major, who objects to Richard's being there and wants him gone. Things are not what they seem as Richard soon learns and the marihuana crop he discovers while repairing fences leads to further drama. In the midst of this, a love affair develops between Rebecca and Richard, adding more problems to his growing list.

Cattle agistment and crop harvesting go hand in hand for the cowboys sent to collect both, but danger looms, and before threats can be fulfilled, Richard decides to act. The demons return and in a fiery conclusion which sees the crop destroyed, the cowboys on the run, and Richard in a life and death situation and in need of answers . . .

Where is Rebecca? Is she, along with the children, safe? Has he once again been fooled and betrayed by a woman?

Conflict of Honour
Copyright © 2019 B.D. Ward
ISBN: 978-1-4874-2537-1
Cover art by Angela Waters

Published by eXtasy Books Inc or
Devine Destinies, an imprint of eXtasy Books Inc

Look for us online at:
www.eXtasybooks.com or www.devinedestinies.com

CONFLICT OF HONOUR

BY

B.D. WARD

DEDICATION

To those who've been there.

CHAPTER ONE

"What's a young colt like you doing in a place like this?" the elderly storekeeper asked, eyeing me off as though I was some sort of rarity.

The leather riding boots, dirty jeans and leather jacket shouldn't have been enough to cause that reaction. It must have been my ruffled hair. The name *Angus* was embroidered on his shirt pocket, and that was all I had by way of introduction.

"You're Angus?" I asked.

He nodded warily. "That's what they call me."

"I'm Richard. I'm looking for work," I replied.

"I've got nothing," he shot back.

"I didn't mean here exactly, but they said at the garage you might know of something in the area."

He scratched his head. "A large number of the young men are away at war at present, which makes things pretty hard in a farming community, but there's bound to be someone needing help." He thought for a moment. "How come you're not over there fighting for your country?" he asked suspiciously.

"It's not a fight for our country. We shouldn't even be there," I told him bitterly. I knew it was a topic that was creating heated debate all over the country.

"You're not one of those draft dodger fellows?"

"I've done my time over there. What about work?" I asked. I didn't want to elaborate any further on my time spent in Vietnam or defend my actions or thoughts on a war that had

1

turned my life upside down.

"You seemed to come out of it unscathed." He looked up and down at this stranger. "Is it as bad as they say it is? Are we winning?"

"Work! Can you help?" I asked. I didn't want to get into a debate with someone that knew nothing except gossip he'd probably picked up at the pub.

"Not really. If you leave your name and a contact number, I can ask around for you. There might be something turn up," he suggested, but the look on his face told me it was most unlikely and he was most disinterested.

"I'm travelling through. No sense in hanging about if there's nothing. Thanks for your help," I said, turning and walking out of the shop, back toward the garage where my motorcycle was parked. I could feel his eyes staring at me as I walked, and felt compelled to turn and stare back, or wave, but resisted. Perhaps my attitude was not the best, but then when your life goes from on top of the world to grovelling in crap, you don't really feel like being friendly and neighbourly to everyone you meet.

Before this useless war, jobs had been plentiful, but now it seemed even the country towns were suffering as much as the cities — not that I was a city person, but since my conscription, I'd lived nowhere else than on the outskirts of large towns or cities. That was until I was shipped out with my battalion for the steamy jungles of that place they called, *hell*.

Australia, they say is, the lucky country? I guess I was one of the lucky ones. At least I came back in one piece, a few scars to remind me of my time there, not wanting to recall anything about the place, and I certainly didn't want to tell what I knew to some shopkeeper who knew nothing more than what he read in the morning paper — government propaganda. Since I'd arrived back, I'd found so much that had been written about the war which painted a different picture to what was actually happening there, but I was free of it now. All I wanted was to get my life back on track.

It wasn't exactly on track before the war. I had planned to be married. She was the girl of my dreams. Eleanor was voluptuous with the broad smile and outrageous humour who could match me or any of my mates, drink for drink. I had a good business I'd started from scratch, but all that faded away the day I received my call-up papers. I had thought about registering as a conscientious objector or anything to delay the inevitable but was told by many I was wasting my time and it was better to go and get it over with. Eleanor and my best mate Tim would look after things while I was away, and when I got back, things could return to normal and life would resume — or that was the plan . . .

Easy for those in authority to say. I was taken halfway around the country for basic training and then to what seemed a world away. Instead of building things, I was now blowing them up, using a rifle instead of a hammer and taking orders instead of giving them. The occasional letters I wrote to Eleanor were always replied to, informing me how things were going at home, but as the months went on, the letters became fewer until they finally stopped altogether.

I wasn't all that worried — more annoyed by not knowing why. There was plenty to do around the base or on patrol, and there was no better place to talk out your problems. There was never a shortage of drinking mates or tall stories, but there was also that worrying edge that each day could be your last. Although that was never talked about openly, it was always in the back of your mind. Skirmishes and ambushes were always on the cards and the VC were quite proficient at setting booby traps in the hope of eliminating one or more of their enemy.

But that was war — kill or be killed, and the first time you press your finger on the trigger and see the flesh tear and blood spurt from your victim reinforces that. You knew it was either him or you. That doesn't make it right, but it gives you the satisfaction in knowing that at least this time, you were lucky. He was your enemy. Someone you didn't know, someone who was there to do the same job as you, only for the other side. The enemy. *Kill or be killed* was a remark used often, especially on patrol, always there in the back of your mind . . . haunting you. Making you suspicious of every noise, every movement around you. Keeping you on your guard.

As cautious as you can be, there is always that moment when time stands still for just a fraction of a second and you realize you are under attack before reflexes and training kick in. By then, if the enemy is accurate, the damage can be done, and those mates you've lived and trained with for what seems a lifetime can be dead. Blown to pieces by some mine, tripped and exploded, or riddled by some automatic weapon fired from the cover of the veiled jungle undergrowth. In some places, it was impenetrable, the perfect place for an enemy to hide. More than once while on patrol we were doused by the fine spray of defoliant as the yanks flew overhead, dropping their orange poison in an attempt to clear the foliage and expose the enemy. It was all part of the job, and we were assured it wouldn't harm us, and besides, orders were orders.

I'd seen it all. Killed many of the enemy and seen my mates die before my eyes, and yet I was here to tell of unspeakable acts. Why? It's people like old Angus who want to know what you did or what you saw, and if you tell him the truth, that look of horror that grips his face and the shaking of his head in disbelief is enough for you to know he doesn't believe a word of what you said. He'll make up his own mind and tell his own story to suit himself and tell it like he believes it happened — even though he hasn't a clue. So why bother? Let him or all of them believe what they like. You had to be there. Was it any wonder my attitude was not the best, but I was working on it?

I kicked the bike into life, the motor burbling away as I took a brief look around before slipping the motorbike into gear and setting off. There was no set direction. There hadn't been since I'd left the hospital after that final checkup. I was free to do what I liked, go where I wanted, and finally, do what I wanted without someone issuing orders and watching over us to ensure they were carried out. I was over that.

The air smelled clean and sweet as I motored along the semi-bitumen country road, keeping to the center to avoid the dropoffs and potholes which were numerous near the sides, before the rough gravel and grass verge. It seemed so peaceful — so heavenly. No traffic, no crowds, just peace and quiet. I slowed the bike. I was in no hurry, I had nowhere to go. The tall gums standing near the road looked inviting and shady, so I pulled off the road and stopped. An hour's rest in the middle of nowhere would do no harm. I took what food and water I had from the saddlebags and sat down in the shade and rested.

In the tranquillity and freshness of the country air, I dozed, then woke to find a young woman walking towards me, the sound of a breaking twig beneath her boot ending my slumber. Through squinting eyes, I watched her come toward me, hair partly showing beneath the hat she wore and the shirt showing stains of sweat while the jeans and boots seemed to be what everyone wore in the country. "Can I help you?" I asked, sitting up, surprising her and bringing her march toward me to a halt.

"I was checking to see if you were all right," she replied. "You don't see too many people at the sides of the road these days unless they've had an accident."

I looked across at the bike which was still standing as I'd left it. "We were just resting."

"Well, if there's no damage, I'll go," she said starting to turn.

"You're from around here?" I asked.

"A few miles up the road. We have a small farm."

"I'm passing through, but also looking for work. You wouldn't know of anything?"

"What can you do?"

I shrugged. "Pretty much whatever I put my hands to work on. I used to be a builder."

"Used to be?" she queried.

"The war intervened."

She nodded as though she understood and eyed me closer.

"Why didn't you go back to building after you returned?"

"Personal reasons," I told her, knowing that meant nothing to her.

"What was it like over there for you?" She came closer, standing a few feet from me.

"A bit different to what you're hearing. It's certainly not a picnic like they say."

"Will we win?"

I shrugged again. "That's anyone's guess. They're a pretty determined bunch we're against. If I had to make a guess, I'd say . . . no."

The smile on her face faded and a look of bewilderment showed. "Are you saying we're losing the war? A lot of good men from around here are there, fighting for their country."

"Don't get upset. You asked me a question and I gave you an answer. It's only my opinion. I'm not an analyst or politician. They're the ones you should be asking," I replied. I wasn't sure if she was offended by my remark. "Do you know some of the men fighting over there?"

"A few. My husband's there."

"Where's he stationed? I might know him." I looked at her more closely, thinking she was no older than myself.

"He's a soldier at some weird-named place. He enlisted."

"What?" I said surprised. "Did he have a death—why would he do that?"

"I didn't want him to, but some of his mates were serving in the army, and his father's a retired Major who fought in the Second World War and then in Korea and felt it was his son's duty to do his bit for Queen and country."

"Queen and country have nothing to do with this war," I told her quietly. "How long has he been there?"

"About eighteen months. He wants to stay on until the end. Until they win."

He must have been a glutton for punishment or one of those who had some cushy office job and never had to sweep through muddied paddy fields or get his hands dirty or bloodied. There were a few of them, but they rarely came onto the base. "Well, let's hope he gets back all right," I finished, hoping to end the discussion and settling back down again against the tree.

"How much do you charge for your services?"

She changed the subject, apparently feeling my opinion on the war differed from hers.

"To do what?" I asked, though with little enthusiasm.

"Odd jobs. Mend fences. Plough." She looked at me curiously.

"That depends, but I'd be happy with a couple of meals a day and a place to sleep."

"Have you mentioned that to anyone else you've spoken to?"

"The conversation had never got that far. You're the first to ask," I replied, thinking of Angus.

"I think that's reasonable. Would you be interested in working for me?"

I took my time considering the proposal, going over in my mind what the work might entail and how hard a boss she might be. I couldn't be sure what was under the hat, but from what I saw, it looked honey-coloured and bundled, but the blouse held back a nicely proportioned torso while the rest of the body sat snugly into the jeans and boots. She waited impatiently for some response. My hesitancy clearly annoyed her and she turned to leave.

"If you're interested at all, my place has the large green gate with the name Greenshaw written on it. The work is there if you want it. If you come in, close the gate after you. I don't want the cattle out on the road." She strode off towards the dilapidated old *Dodge* truck she was driving.

She stopped, turned and gave me another look before getting in, starting the truck and driving off. I watched as she drove away, wondering how it was I hadn't heard her arrive with the noise the holey muffler was making. Since Vietnam, I'd become a light sleeper, waking at the sound of a pin drop, usually — but since Vietnam, sleep had been a constant problem anyway. I stood up and stretched, feeling my body creak and crack, then relax. The best thing about working this way was that if I didn't like it or things became overbearing, I could up and leave, nothing lost except time.

I moved over to the bike and put the drink and remainder of the food into the saddlebags and straddled the machine. It had been years since I'd worked for a boss — not counting the army of course, where you had bosses — a chain of command.

I was fifteen and straight from school when I started my apprenticeship in carpentry with a local builder. At first it had been a slog, but I enjoyed the work. When my time was up, I started my own business and watched it grow. I sighed, thinking over what should have been — what could have been.

I kicked the bike into life. "This should be interesting," I told myself and drove steadily onto the roadway. The truck was out of sight, but she'd given me the directions, so all I had to do was follow them. Where they were likely to lead, I was unsure, but the way my life had been going, it certainly couldn't be any worse.

Chapter Two

The gate was easily seen from the road, with its bright green paint and black lettering hand painted on the top rail. I did as she asked and closed the gate after entering, looking at the winding track ahead of me, wondering how large the property actually was. The ruts from the truck were clearly marked and deep and treacherous for the wheels of the bike, so I stayed alongside them as they wound round rough ground, down hills and through a small shallow creek with placid water before rising up and around another hill, where a large house sat predominantly on the crest.

The *Dodge* was around the back of the house, parked where it stopped between the house and a large barn. The place looked deserted. If I hadn't spoken with the woman only minutes before and watched her drive away in the utility, I might have thought there was no one about. I cut the motor and kicked down the stand, then got off the bike. It was undulating country, and this appeared to be one of the highest points, looking prominently over much of the surrounding area. There were cattle grazing on the lush pastures and what looked like corn or some other crop growing in a small paddock.

Two dogs came onto the verandah and barked at me — a brown Kelpie and a blue cattle dog, sounding the alarm that some stranger had entered their territory. With no one bothering to come from the house, I made my way across and walked up the few stairs to the verandah which surrounded the house. Both dogs growled and backed away as I did so, but made no attempt to attack me. I was about to knock on the door when it opened enough for a young boy to look suspiciously up at me.

"What do you want?"

His hand was still holding the door handle as though ready to shut it in my face if he felt the need.

"Would the lady that was driving that truck a few minutes ago be at home?" I asked pointing to the vehicle so there'd be no misunderstanding.

"Mum?"

He looked at the truck, then at me.

"I'll go and see. Sit down, Blue!" he commanded the cattle dog, but both dogs obeyed.

He closed the door before I could answer and I heard him rush off and yell out to his mother. I wasn't sure of his age, perhaps seven or eight, which meant she must have been a child bride when she had him if my calculations of her age were correct. Then again, looks can be deceiving.

The door opened again and she stood there, a smirk on her face. This time the hat was missing and that honey-coloured hair hung down to her shoulders. The face was more visible and lovelier than I had thought at first.

"You found the place all right?"

"I'm here, aren't I?"

"I somehow had my doubts you'd show, but I've been wrong before."

The young boy pushed forward around his mother to get a better look at me before another child appeared—a girl, younger than the boy, pushed her way through.

"You've met Toby." The woman's hand went to the head of the boy and she rubbed it lovingly. "And this is Helen," she added, doing the same with the girl.

I nodded to them both. "I'm Richard."

"We never did introduce ourselves," she recalled. "I'm

Rebecca."

"Nice name." I looked around a little uneasy, the dogs still giving a gurgling growl, but remaining as they'd been told. "Where do I bunk, and what would you like me to do?" I asked.

She put her hand on my shoulder and moved out onto the verandah, turning me and walking across with me, the children following, their curiosity aroused.

"You can bunk down in the barn. There's plenty of room, but you might have to clear some of the junk out of the way. There's water connected for washing and drinking, but if you want to bathe, over the back, there's a small dam that's ideal for swimming and fishing."

"Is he going to stay here?" Toby asked.

"He's going to be helping out about the place," his mother told him.

"But I can do that. Dad left me in charge when he went. Why do we need help?"

He now arrogantly eyed me off with some disdain.

"You're still in charge Toby, but Richard will be doing the work that you and I can't or don't have the time for," she attempted to explain.

"I can do everything. Dad said I could."

He looked at me in a disgruntled fashion.

"You have school. Your father would be happier if your grades improved and there was someone bigger and stronger helping about the place," she said attempting to make my presence easier to understand.

"I'll bet Granddad won't be happy." He sulked.

"I'll worry about that. Now both of you go in and get cleaned up for dinner."

Turning back to me she asked, "Do you think you can sort yourself out over there?"

"Probably a lot easier than you're going to be able to sort

him out," I replied as I watched Toby take the hand of his sister and go back inside. "Who's Granddad?"

"Geoffrey's father. The Major. He visits occasionally to keep an eye on the place. It's nothing for you to worry about."

I wondered.

"Well, I'll go and sort out my new quarters," I said, stepping off the verandah onto the stairs.

"You can come over for dinner in about an hour, if that suits?"

"I'm sure it will." I stepped down to the ground and walked across to my bike, kicking away the stand and pushing it towards the barn and inside.

She was right, in that there was plenty of room and also an enormous amount of what could only be described as junk. An old tractor sat in one corner, partly covered with straw and dust with the disc plough still connected, but rusting like other attachments not far away. Old furniture, some good, while some only fit for burning or dumping, seemed to be everywhere. A workbench attached itself along one wall with a myriad of tools, and lubricants all covered with dust were just waiting for the day when they, too, could be cleaned and made use of as they were meant to be.

I shook my head. The barn seemed to be the only thing that was in reasonable condition, but then I hadn't looked too closely. I wasn't sure what Rebecca wanted from me, but there was enough work in the barn to keep me busy for months. I propped the bike and took a closer look. Some bales of hay were stacked against one wall, but hadn't been needed for some time and were slowly falling apart, scattering the dried straw throughout the barn anytime the wind blew through the open doors at either end. I checked the doors at one end and found they closed, but not cleanly, as the hinges were stretched.

An old divan covered with straw and dust seemed a likely

bed for the night as I pulled it from the junk and set about brushing it down, filling the room with dust. I coughed and laughed. "What a joke," I told myself, going back and opening the doors I'd just closed. The Kelpie barked as though agreeing with me, although I hadn't noticed him before. "Hope I'm not stealing your room," I told him, the dog keeping his distance. As the dust cleared, I went back and continued cleaning until I was satisfied I could sleep comfortably on the divan without suffocating every time I rolled over. An old kerosene lamp was the only means of lighting, and I checked to see if that worked — which it did, so I was slowly getting my living quarters organised.

The time passed quickly as the darkness came upon me without my realising, and Toby came from the house to tell me that his mother said my dinner was ready. I hadn't cleaned up and looked as dusty and dilapidated as most of the junk in the barn, but made an effort to clean myself with a wash basin and jug of water, throwing on a clean shirt before going over to the house.

My first impressions of the house — or the rooms I saw — was that it was a gentleman's residence, going by the older style, but in excellent condition were the furnishings and memorabilia that cluttered the rooms. Family photographs and pictures of men in uniform adorned the walls and sat over the mantle of the fireplace in the lounge room, while the dining room contained just a few photographs, and on closer inspection, I saw they were all taken of Rebecca and her family at some recent time.

Rebecca had told me to sit myself down and she would bring in the dinner as she watched me scrutinising the photographs. I turned and looked towards the table and saw that Toby had positioned himself at the head while his sister and Rebecca sat on either side. He watched me as I pulled out the chair and sat down next to his sister.

"Mum said you've been at the war. My father's there at present. Do you know him?"

I shook my head and looked over at the picture of the uniformed soldier standing to attention. "No. He was probably in another section of the forces."

"Granddad says he's going to be a General one day," he said with some authority.

"Those sorts of things take time," I told him, unsure what he'd been told.

Helen spoke up for the first time. "Granddad says he'll help."

"I'm sure he will."

"How is it you came home? Didn't you like it there?" Toby continued.

"I'd seen enough. They didn't need my help anymore." I had no wish to go into any details of my past conflict with a seven-year-old.

"We are winning, then. Granddad says we are."

I had no wish to continue the conversation, and luckily Rebecca came through with a large pot which she set down on a folded towel and set about ladling the contents of the pot onto our plates.

"It's only a stew, but there are vegetables in it, so it's quite filling."

I nodded, taking the plate gratefully, since it was the first home cooked meal I'd had in a long time.

"I hope Toby hasn't been boring you with war talk. That's all he and his grandfather talk about when he's here."

"There were a few questions which I hope I handled satisfactorily," I answered, hoping I'd heard the last of it.

"Why didn't you like it there?" Toby asked again.

"I don't think Richard wants to talk about the war now, Toby. Eat your dinner," Rebecca said, coming to my rescue again.

I smiled and nodded to her, grateful for the help.

"You're getting yourself comfortable in the barn?"

"I've been in worse spots," I replied, a grin on my face.

"I can imagine."

"The old tractor and machinery. What's the —"

"I doubt any of that stuff works. Geoffrey put it in there before he left, and that's where it's stayed. The paddocks with the corn and lucerne we dug by hand. Not real successfully, but we managed. Toby and Helen helped," she added, praising the two children.

"While I'm cleaning up in the barn, would you like me to look at those few things?"

"If you think you can, that would be a great help, but the priority at present would be to mend a few of the fences around the property."

"How many head of cattle do you have?" I asked, having seen a few that afternoon on the drive up to the house.

"Actually none. A friend of the Major's brings them here to fatten up before going to the markets. He pays us agistment fees to look after the cattle, which isn't a lot, but it all helps. I suppose there is a couple of hundred head scattered about."

I was surprised she knew so little about what cattle were there but guessed she had enough with the children and keeping the place running reasonably smoothly. "The Major visits regularly?"

"He comes and goes. This place used to be his, but he talked Geoffrey into buying it and he moved closer to the city so he could keep his eye on things."

I looked at her with a puzzled expression.

"He might be retired, but he still has friends in the army. He feels it can't run without him, so he's always hanging around giving advice. I'm not sure they take it, but he seems to be well informed about what goes on."

"Was Geoffrey a farmer?"

She chuckled. "He was the son of an army man, used to being shunted about the country. He tried his hand at a number of things before the Major got his way and talked him into enlisting. Whether it was the Major, or Geoffrey, my husband found something that he loved doing, I wasn't sure, but promotions came his way more easily than anything he'd ever put his hand to. We both knew nothing about the land or farming when we came here, and then he left and got posted overseas, leaving me completely lost."

"Then why would you come here?"

"It was at the request of the Major. He'd had the place for some time and didn't use it a lot and thought maybe Geoffrey would find it interesting."

"Interesting? Farming is a lot of hard work if it's done properly. Long hours and—"

"You don't have to tell me. I know. The place is starting to get run down, and I can't do a lot about it. That's why I asked you for help." She gave me an exasperated, pleading look.

I stared at her blankly. "I'm not a farmer either. I find it strange that someone who knows nothing about this life would choose to live here. Alone. Out of the way. You must miss the city life—your friends?"

"I have the children. And the Major visits, and there are friends from town and the school. The loneliness you get used to. Besides, most of my friends are scattered all over the place, anyway. That's what happens when you're traveling a lot."

I was sure she smiled more for the benefit of the children.

"So, how do you survive?" I asked, hoping I wasn't getting too personal.

"I get an allowance from Geoffrey, and there are the agistment fees, and if I do run short, the Major helps out, but I try to avoid his help if I can," she answered, though there seemed a certain frustration in her voice.

"Why? I'd be grateful for any help."

"Don't get me wrong, I am, but he has the habit of being a bit overbearing at times, as though he's still in the army and he still owns this place. He forgets himself."

She looked away from me as she spoke, but I had the feeling there was much more she wasn't telling.

"Anyway, enough about me, what about you — the builder and soldier? What's your story?"

Her attitude changed and she seemed pleased that she was about to hear my story, letting her off the hook for telling more about her.

"I don't really have one, and what I have would only bore you and not be fit for dinner conversation anyway," I told her, avoiding telling her anymore. "What's the Kelpie's name?"

"Red!" Toby called out, returning to the conversation.

"And Blue," Helen joined in. "He won't hurt you."

"No. I had Red settling in over at the barn. I hope I'm not pinching his bed," I said, grinning at her.

"He sleeps anywhere," she replied.

"And with anyone, so watch out," Rebecca warned jokingly. She rose from the table, taking some of the dirty dishes through to the kitchen before returning to check on the children. "It's time for bed," she told them both to the groans and objections they replied with. "Get into your pyjamas and I'll be in shortly to tuck you both in."

Reluctantly the children got up from the table, looking forlornly towards me before walking off into another room. "Would you like a hand to wash up?" I asked as she cleared away the dishes.

"No. You have enough to do. You can take the ute in the morning if you want."

"The bike might be easier until I know what I'm up against. Is there much to be repaired?"

"I don't really know. I've never checked it. The Major had a look at one time, and I recall Geoffrey doing the same, but there have been a few cattle get out lately, so there must be a break somewhere," she said, walking me to the door.

I walked onto the verandah, where the two dogs were lying.

"Take Red with you if you like. He seems to have made some attachment with you."

As she spoke, the Kelpie got up, looking at me as though waiting for some command.

"The kids won't mind?"

"Blue's their favourite. He watches them like a hawk."

She smiled at me and I nodded, then turned and went down the stairs, the Kelpie moving quietly behind me. I'd left the lantern turned on to guide me to the divan and sat down wondering what I'd got myself into. There was no doubt Rebecca needed help, but just how much, and how much I could offer, was something I wouldn't know until I'd seen just how rundown this property appeared to be. I lay back on the divan and looked up at the roof thinking I had at least some protection from the weather for a change, though whether that would make any difference to my sleep was yet to be determined. I said goodnight to Red and turned on my side and hoped the demons of my past would let me sleep.

CHAPTER THREE

The sunlight was creeping slowly into the barn when I woke, Red yawning and stretching out on the ground beside the divan. I sat up, my back feeling like I'd laid on some lumpy hard ground all night and needed to be straightened out. I think it was more likely the fact that this was the first night for some time I'd slept on a soft, comfortable surface. I stood up and stretched, feeling my bones creak and crack, before setting about making a start for the day.

I checked the saddlebags and made sure I had water and food for the day, then went to the workbench and inspected what tools were there. Wire cutters, stretchers, axe and numerous implements that might be handy, along with a roll of wire for fixing any damaged areas. I loaded all I could onto the bike and looked over at Red. "You coming? It's likely to be a long day." He nodded as though he understood and walked out of the barn. I straddled the bike and went through the motions, ensuring I made as little noise as possible and idled the bike out, past the utility and down the hill before opening the throttle. To my surprise Red was running along beside me, keeping pace with the speed I was doing.

I started at the entrance, the green gate, and followed the fence along, taking my time and allowing Red to stay with me. There were places where the posts were leaning, but nothing that would allow the cattle to get out. There were places that the shrubs and lantana had grown wild and covered the fence, but there were still no visible signs that the cattle could get through. It was not until midmorning that I found a break. As insignificant as it was, it was still enough to allow any inquisitive cow the opportunity to wander through, and I guessed if one led the others would follow.

The land was virgin country that had never been touched except for the surveying and the fence, and that was probably many years before. I still found it remarkable that Rebecca knew nothing about the property except for the driveway and around the house. I wondered if she'd ever taken the time to explore any of the ground. The cattle roamed freely, staying in groups, feeding on the lush grasses and taking shelter from the sun under the abundance of shade trees. Some watched me with curiosity as I repaired the break, unconcerned their only chance of escape was now thwarted. Red, in turn, watched them, making sure their curiosity didn't bring them too close to us and at the ready to repel any aggressive advance.

The country was by no means reminiscent of the jungles of Vietnam, but there were places where a sudden flashback to something that had happened on patrol brought my actions to a sudden halt and made me wary of the surroundings. But that was all in my mind, playing tricks. My demons playing games with me. It was peaceful here. Not a sound of gunfire, choppers or mortars — just birds, insects . . . and peace.

Another mile or so, I found another break, though there were no cattle to watch the repair this time, just Red keeping an eager eye on what was about. The sun was high and I guessed it was near noon when I stopped for what I considered a well-earned rest in an area thickly overgrown and not far from the creek that appeared to meander through the property. I removed my shirt and washed, the cool waters washing away the sweat from the morning's work, then settled down in the shade and shared a biscuit with Red.

I was glad I'd taken the bike, as the utility wouldn't have covered half the ground or got into many of the tight places the bike had, and walking up and down hills would have made the job twice as difficult. I relaxed and let my mind wander, thinking of my past life, the building, the war and now this. What next? It was clear Rebecca had little money, although, from the way she spoke, her husband should have been sending her enough. Then there was the Major and the agistment fees. Perhaps she wasn't being told everything. Perhaps she was being treated like a mushroom and kept in the dark about the money. I'd been there and done that and didn't like to see it happen to someone as nice as Rebecca. She seemed vague about anything to do with the farm.

I looked at my watch and gave Red a playful pat on the head, waking him from a tranquil rest. He grunted and looked up. "Time to get back to work," I told him. He stood up and shook himself, then went to the creek where he lapped at the water a few times before returning to the bike. "Do you think you could sit there?" I indicated the pillion seat and without a blink, he jumped up on the seat and shuffled to get comfortable. I wasn't sure he'd stay there once I started the bike, but there was one way to find out. I took my time, driving steadily along the fence line, feeling Red bump against me as I turned or slowed, but found him to be as stable as any passenger I'd carried before.

By three that afternoon, I'd covered about halfway around the property and decided to return to the barn and continue the checking of the fence the next day. There were no tracks or trails through the property I'd seen, so I set out to follow the creek back to the homestead, knowing that the house and barn would be visible as I got closer. With Red sitting snugly behind me I followed the twists and turns and passed stretches of water that flowed over the shallows like rapids at times, making it a wonderful playground for any person seeking a wet adventure.

As I rounded the bank at a place where the creek widened

out, I was surprised to see a metal shed not far from the bank nestled back into the foliage and under the cover of the overhanging trees. I slowed the bike and stopped, having heard no mention of any shed from Rebecca. It was miles from anywhere, and unless Geoffrey had built it as a getaway, it seemed strange that it was even there. I propped the bike and hopped off, Red following me as I walked over to take a closer look. The metal door was shut but not locked, as a turn of the handle proved. I looked inside. The daylight from the open door and the small window at the side showed an assortment of digging and cutting tools, a small generator and a number of fuel tins.

"Do we have a poacher living here?" I asked Red, who was noncommittal. "Why would anyone be out here in the middle of nowhere, with all this?" I was sure Rebecca would have mentioned the shed if she knew it was there. I was curious. I could think of a number of possibilities, most of which were not legal, but that was my mentality from Vietnam. I closed the door and looked around. An old campfire that hadn't been used for some time was still visible, given the small pile of charcoal on the ground and a track leading into the heavily timbered bushland behind the shed was not yet overgrown. "What do you think, Red, should we go for a snoop?"

I'm sure if he'd answered, he'd have said *After you*, as he waited for me to lead the way along the track. I was not that far in when I found what I suspected—a crop of marijuana, extending throughout the trees and bushland. Some of the plants were as tall as me, reaching up for the sunlight that filtered through from the trees and overhanging branches.

"Well, Red, who says the farm isn't productive?" I asked the dog as he cocked his leg and urinated against the stalk of one of the plants. "I wonder who's responsible for this little enterprise." I moved through the plants, unable to calculate how large the crop was, but guessing it was considerable.

Some of the plants were starting to flower, letting off that unmistakable odour and telling that they were ready for harvesting. "I can't see this being allowed to go to waste," I told Red, who still had that disinterested look on his face. "So I wonder what happens now. Someone will have to do something about it soon."

For the area that the crop covered and the size of the plants, it was obvious that they had been looked after, but by whom? It was big business in Vietnam—drugs, and marijuana especially—enough for a person to forget their troubles without becoming too addicted. It seemed at some time everyone up there was on something. It was no wonder the war was going to the dogs. I'd tried it, like most of the men in our company, but I didn't become reliant on it like some did, paying large amounts of money just so they could forget the reality of what was happening around them.

I made my way back to the shed, Red on my heels, racing back to the bike and jumping back on the seat. I looked about. Whoever was growing this had to be coming in from somewhere, and from what I'd seen today, there was no access in for vehicles at any place along the fence. Maybe I'd find out more tomorrow. I got back on the bike and slowly moved along the bank, keeping my eyes open for any signs which might give me some idea of how they, whoever they were, were getting to the crop, although with the rain and the time since they were last there unknown, it was like looking for a needle in a haystack.

My thoughts turned to Rebecca and whether she knew. It would certainly make the farm productive, but that wasn't the picture she painted of the place. I'd already been deceived by one woman. Though that was entirely a different matter, I didn't want it to become a habit. I could drop subtle hints over dinner, telling her what I'd found and see how she reacted. That was one thing I could do. Another was to say nothing and let things run their course. I certainly didn't want any trouble with her or the local police, but I was curious as to who was responsible.

Some distance further on, I came across a large split-post pen, the yard used for holding the cattle before loading them onto the transport to be taken away. After seeing some of the country the cattle were roaming in, I wondered what was used to round them up and get them back to the yard, and looking at the ruts in the ground, what transport was used to carry the cattle out. Surely Rebecca had some idea about that?

Another mile or so downstream, I saw the house and barn on the hill and noticed the dam Rebecca had spoken about. It was roughly built, with rocks blocking the creek until the water expanded and rose to the point where it again flowed over the rocky barrier and continued on its way. I stopped the bike and dismounted, Red following me to the water's edge, curious. I picked up a stick and threw it towards the hill and he instinctively turned and chased it. While he was retrieving it, I checked the water out seeing how cool and clear it looked — inviting after a hot day's work.

Red brought back the stick and dropped it at my feet. I picked it up and tossed it into the water. Without thinking, the dog took an almighty leap into the water and started swimming towards the floating stick. "If it's good enough for you, then it's good enough for me," I told him and quickly undressed and ran into the water, letting my body sink into the cool waters and relax. Not to be outdone, Red brought the stick back to me dropping it in the water and nudging it against me waiting for me to throw it again. It seemed it was a game he could play all day on land or water, but for me, it was a means of having a quick wash, and after a moment's drying, getting dressed and hopping back on the bike again. This time Red opted to run alongside as I made my way up the hill towards the barn.

On my arrival, the first thing I noticed was the gold Mercedes parked near the old Dodge. I wondered who the visitor might be. With the light slowly fading, I parked the bike in the barn and lit the lamp for the night. I'd been there only a few minutes when Toby came in, Red giving a warning growl that someone was approaching.

"Where were you all day?" he asked authoritatively.

"Checking and repairing the fences," I replied, knowing I was taking his work from him.

"Mum said you can come for dinner when you're ready, and dress re . . . spe . . . spect . . . fully."

He stumbled over the word *respectfully*, as much as I was mystified why he said it. Surely Rebecca hadn't asked for it, knowing the limited wardrobe I carried. The jeans were still damp from the dip I'd taken, but the shirt was dry and still showed signs of the sweat stains from the day's work. It needed washing, as did most of the other clothes I had in the saddlebags. "I'll do my best," I said, not interested in burdening him with my problems. I pointed to the gold Mercedes. "Who's driving the Merc?"

"Granddad. He's come to check on you." He turned and hurried back to the house, leaving me to wonder what was in store for me over there. It was the way Toby said *check on you* that made me hesitant. A seven-year-old doesn't speak like that unless he's heard it come from the mouth of someone older, and I wasn't interested in some retired Major digging about in my past.

I made myself as *respectable* as possible, did my hair, and strutted across to the house, looking forward to whatever Rebecca had cooked for dinner and nothing more. I climbed the stairs onto the verandah and knocked on the door and waited.

Rebecca opened it and gave me a curt smile. "Sorry about this, but we have a visitor. Toby phoned him this morning without me knowing and told him about you. He's come up to find out about you. If you don't want to do this, I'll tell him you're not well, but he'll still want to talk to you. He's wary of strangers, especially with Geoffrey away."

"I've nothing to hide as long as he doesn't get too personal." I decided to change the subject. "What's on the menu?" I grinned, letting her know I was hungry.

She opened the door wider and allowed me to step inside — much like the spider would for the fly.

CHAPTER FOUR

The two children were sitting together at the table, the head being taken by the stern-faced man who was talking with them as we entered. He stopped talking and looked closely at me.

"John. Major. This is Richard," Rebecca said, making the introduction.

He started to stand as I made my way around the table and held out my hand. He shook hands firmly as he sat back, realising he'd made a mistake in standing, then released my hand as though he'd touched something he quickly regretted.

"Rebecca tells me you're looking for work?" he said, a look of disapproval on his face.

He was dressed in a long-sleeved white shirt and dark pants, the coat of which I saw hanging over the back of his chair when he partly stood. Immaculate. Perhaps that was the reason for the disapproving look when he saw my attire. I guessed he was in his sixties or thereabouts and had that look of authority which oozed from the way he sat and stared. The tanned and lined face and the now receding hairline had seen their share of sunshine and inclement weather, I guessed, and the small but noticeable moustache gave him that look of an army officer from yesteryear.

"I have been, but she's kindly offered to let me help her out on the farm," I said, pulling out my chair to sit as Rebecca went back to the kitchen.

"The place needs little doing to it. Besides, what there is, I think young Toby here can handle," he said rubbing the head of the boy who squirmed slightly beneath his touch.

"From what I've seen so far, it would take more than a seven-year-old to fix some of the smaller problems the property has," I replied with some certainty.

"Nevertheless, your services are not wanted around here," he replied adamantly.

"I think Rebecca would be the best judge of that," I retorted, trying hard not to sound too mordant.

"The best judge of what?" Rebecca asked. She had just returned from the kitchen, placing a plate of food in front of the Major and one each in front of Toby and his sister.

"I was just saying the place was *not* in need of a handyman," the Major answered, stressing his argument.

Rebecca shook her head. "I beg to differ. There are a number of —"

"Let the boy handle them." The Major looked over at Toby and gave a wry smile. "He's the man of the house while his father's away."

"He can't, Major. He's only a boy," Rebecca objected.

"Rubbish! What's he been doing all day anyway?" he shot back, staring at me as though I was some irritating pest waiting to be stomped on or swatted.

"Mending fences," I answered. I was not interested in getting into a family squabble, but I was also not interested in being treated like some layabout by the former Major.

"I asked Richard to check the fences. Some of the cattle have been getting out and wandering," Rebecca told him.

"When? Why didn't you tell me?" he asked, looking at her, disgruntled.

"I have . . . a few times. I didn't want to lose any or have them killed. They're not ours."

I admired the way she stood up for herself, but it was like hitting your head against a brick wall as the Major either rebuked or dismissed her claims.

"I know. I could have got Charlie to send some of his boys down to check on them and the fences. You don't need to have any extra help here," the Major said as she went back to the kitchen. She returned with another two plates, one for me and the other for her.

I was about to tuck in when the Major started to say *Grace*.

"For what we are about to receive . . ."

For a time, only the clunking of metal on china was heard as the meal was eaten, though there were numerous stares around the table, as though waiting for something to be said.

"You've just returned from Vietnam," the Major said finally breaking the silence.

"He doesn't know my father," Toby broke in.

"Of course not. Your father's an officer," the Major told him, arrogantly looking at me as though expecting a response. "How long have you been out of the service?"

"About six months ago," I replied. I didn't want to divulge too much, but I also knew he had the ability and the contacts to find out all about me.

"Six months with nothing to do," he mused, as though his assumption that I was a waste of space had been vindicated.

"Three months in hospital and rehabilitation gave me plenty to do before I spent a month sorting out my personal life, then going on the road."

"And you ended up here."

"It could have been anywhere. I got on the bike and drove. Regardless of what you think, there's not a lot of work about at present." I could feel my voice lifting as I became angry. The children were turning their heads as though watching a tennis match between two players, as the exchanges between the Major and myself continued.

"It's there if you like to look," he replied arrogantly.

"I *was* looking. I thought I'd found work," I shot back, looking beside me to Rebecca.

"You have," Rebecca said defiantly. "Major, you know I can't handle everything that has to be done here. When Geoffrey was here, he was pushed to get done what was needed. And since that time, the place has gone backward. If it keeps falling apart the way it is, there'll be nothing left by the time Geoffrey returns."

"That's rubbish! If you need extra help, you only had to ask. Taking someone off the street, someone you don't know. You run an awful risk."

"What are you saying?" I asked indignantly.

"What unit were you with and where were you stationed up there?"

He asked something I had expected long before this.

"I don't see we have to discuss any of this in front of the children, Major," Rebecca blurted out, receiving another dark look from the Major.

"Certainly. We'll finish the meal and continue later. On the verandah."

When he said *on the verandah*, he was looking directly at me as though we'd just agreed to some nineteenth century duelling contest—guns at the ready and twenty paces—commence.

After that, the dinner seemed a blur. Rebecca finally stood, telling the children it was time for bed. The Major also stood, looking coldly towards me, then wandering off to the coolness of the verandah. I sat, listening to the talking and laughter of the children for a while until Rebecca returned and started to clear away the dishes.

"I'll help you with that," I told her, getting up and starting to help, but she declined.

"No. He's waiting for you on the verandah. Don't take any guff from him. He enjoys bullying people," she said quietly, looking towards the doorway that led to the verandah.

"I won't be bullied. How desperate are you that I stay?" I

asked in an attempt to establish some boundaries, as well as further keep him waiting.

"I'd appreciate your help, if that's what you're asking," she replied.

"Good enough for me," I answered and made my way through to the verandah.

The Major was leaning on the rail looking out into the darkness, puffing on a large cigar. He turned to me as I walked out, blowing smoke towards my face.

"Those things will kill you," I told him, dodging the plume of smoke and walking around him.

"Never. They're the best. Cuban," he shot back, making a mockery of my suggestion.

"I know what they are, and they'll still kill you."

"You don't smoke?"

"I did in Vietnam, but not now."

"Do drugs?" he asked casually.

I hesitated. "I knew plenty who did."

"So what company were you with?" he continued, returning to the reason we were both there.

"I was at Nui Dat," I told him and he seemed impressed.

"You saw your share of action, then?"

"We had our fair share."

"She doesn't need your help, you know," he said, quickly changing the subject, as though overruling Rebecca's decision while she was not about.

"From what I've seen, she *does* need help, and plenty of it," I contradicted. For the short time I'd been there and from what I'd seen, she was in desperate need.

"I can get her all the help she needs."

"Then why haven't you? You know she's struggling."

"Rubbish. She gets an allowance from Geoffrey, and there are the cattle," the Major mussed.

"That doesn't repair the machinery and plant the crops. I

repaired the fence in a couple of places and there could still be more. How would your friend feel about his cattle getting out and being killed or stolen?"

He huffed and took a long slow draw on the cigar. "How long do you intend to be around?"

I felt like answering, *permanently*, just to piss him off some more, but I was trying to avoid an all-out fight between us. "For as long as she needs me. Without having a good look about, I'd say there's more than a couple of months work here."

"When Geoffrey hears about this, he won't be too pleased."

"Perhaps he should have stayed at home," I answered. I guessed it wouldn't be too long now before Geoffrey heard the news.

He let out a growling sound and looked daggers at me. "You're a confounded nuisance. How much do you want to leave?"

That took me by surprise. "Money?"

"What else? I don't want you around here. It doesn't look good. There's a certain image to uphold."

"What are you saying?"

"I think you know what I'm getting at. You being here is going to wreck Rebecca's reputation as a married woman."

"Now *you're* talking rubbish. Is there something going on you don't want me to know about, or are you just being bloody-minded?" I asked, really becoming annoyed.

"I'm looking after my son's interests — how much?" he persisted, blowing cigar smoke in my direction again.

"I'm afraid Rebecca's my boss, and until she tells me otherwise, I'd like to remind you I'm not in the army anymore and I don't take orders from the likes of you. Now, if we have nothing more to discuss, I might hit the sack. It's been a long day," I said stepping onto the steps and down to the ground.

"Think over what I said. If you won't do it for money or

me, think about Rebecca and the kids. Geoffrey is over there fighting a war for his country, not knowing what is happening back here. The locals wouldn't take kindly to a stranger messing about with one of their own. There is a matter of honour at stake here. In the army, we're all brothers — mates. There's a bond between us all. Something that can't be broken, regardless of what you think of me, think about him — and her."

I briefly looked at him, then walked across the ground to the barn, feeling his knifing gaze on me the whole way. If he was appealing to my sense of loyalty, he would need a better argument than he'd put up. Some of my *brothers — mates —* were dead and many were still recovering, while those that were still fighting would remain in my thoughts, should we ever meet up again. If Geoffrey worked in Admin, he knew more than most about what was going on and was well away from any danger or fighting. No doubt the Major had seen to that.

I took off my shirt and lay down on the sofa, noticing that Red was at my side. I dropped my hand down and patted him gently on the head, bringing a tiresome yawn from my new companion. "At least I've made one friend." I chuckled, letting him settle down for the night. My thoughts filtered back to the marijuana crop and who might be responsible. I hadn't had the chance to query Rebecca, but it did strike me strange that the Major was so insistent that he didn't want me around. Was he really worried about his daughter-in-law's reputation, or perhaps his own? Whose honour was he referring to? There was still a stigma around divorce and broken marriages. Although it was becoming more accepted these days, I had no wish to be responsible for breaking up a happy family.

The thoughts that the Major might be involved with the crop did ring some bells, but why would a man of his standing want to be involved in that seedy side of life? He was retired and I guessed on a good pension. He drove a good vehicle and, without asking, I guessed he lived at some upper-class address in the city. He had no need of any pursuits of this kind, which left me wondering how and where those responsible entered and removed the crop without Rebecca or the Major knowing? Or did they know?

Tomorrow I'd leave early again and continue checking the fence, and if I had time I'd return to the crop and have a second look. I heard Red growl and glanced over at the shadow which entered and moved towards us.

"Are you still awake?" Rebecca asked as she stopped short of Red, who had settled again knowing who it was.

"Just daydreaming. You shouldn't be here," I told her.

"The Major's gone to bed and the children are asleep. What happened between you two?"

"Nothing, really. Just a lot of hot air. He doesn't want me around, but I told him I was working for you and wouldn't be going anywhere until I got my marching orders directly from you."

"Good. He didn't say too much when he came in. I took it things hadn't gone his way and he wasn't in a good mood. I brought you some eats in case you're not about at breakfast. You surprised me leaving so early this morning."

"I had a lot to do." I reached over and took the package from her without getting off the sofa. "I should finish the fencing tomorrow, unless I find a bad section. Do you ever go into the hills and check your property?" I hedged.

"What for? There's enough to do around here without looking for more," she replied, as though her whole world only revolved around the house and children.

"Does anyone ever go bush and check?"

"Some of the boys when they round up the cattle. They have a yard somewhere there where they load and unload the beasts, but I've never worried about going there. They keep to themselves and never come up to the house."

"Is that right? When are they expected again?" I asked, the dim light of ideas in my mind becoming brighter.

"I'm not sure, but I guess sometime soon."

"They don't tell you they're coming?" It was unbelievable how much Rebecca didn't know about what went on around the farm.

"Usually the Major tells me. His friend lets him know. I've never had anything to do with it."

"They bring cattle in and take cattle out and you've never seen them or had anything to do with them?" I said, settling back on the sofa. "That's interesting."

"It's difficult raising two small children without a father and trying to run a farm and do everything, Richard," she said in an exasperated tone.

I hadn't meant to sound condescending. "I think you're doing a good job—and thanks for the eats, they'll come in handy."

"Goodnight," she said and turned and walked out of the barn.

"Goodnight—and thanks again," I muttered, though I doubt she heard me. It was the end of day one, and I couldn't believe all the dramas that unfolded. At least I had Rebecca and Red on my side, but I was probably in for a long and grubby spar with the Major. At least we both knew where we stood. I didn't like his authoritative standover tactics, and he didn't like me being around. Just how it would play out remained to be seen, but so long as I had Rebecca siding with me, I felt I had a commanding chance of retaining my employment—in the short term, at least.

CHAPTER FIVE

The place was quiet when Red and I made an early exit from the barn the following morning, the food Rebecca had brought tucked in the saddle bag with the depleted stock of my own. I went past the yards and the small hut which fronted the crop and drove on to where I had finished the day before, then began the tedious job of moving steadily along the fence line looking for any further breaks.

It was another warm day, but I did notice the buildup of clouds to the west, a sure sign of a storm later in the day, or at least the chance of rain that night. Red sat behind me most of the time, though when the going got rough, he found it easier and quicker to jump off and make his own way around the offending obstacle and let me flounder about without him to worry about. There was the noted absence of cattle in this area, but that could be because of the steep and treacherous slopes, which were more than a handful for me to manoeuvre the bike on. But the fences in this area were all intact, though there seemed little need for them, other than to align the property.

By noon, we were nearing the end of our journey, the green gate coming into sight, and although the journey had been arduous, there had been nothing much to repair. I stopped the bike and settled under a tree and opened the saddlebag that contained our lunch. Red waited patiently while I unwrapped what Rebecca had prepared. Meat sandwiches, much the same as Toby would have taken in his lunchbox to school, a welcome change from the biscuits from yesterday, and readily devoured by both Red and myself. After that, we both settled for a restful sleep under the shade of the tree with a gentle breeze making it more appealing.

Sleep for me had not been restive for some time. There was always something. A failed love life. The war. The business. The killing and the loss of mates . . . always something. And now, the thought that Rebecca, an innocent woman, might be unknowingly having her property used for growing drugs in large quantities. I couldn't be sure what the penalty for getting caught with such a crop might be, but I guessed it would be substantial, and for a woman with two small children, devastating. I sighed, shuffling my back against the tree trunk thinking about the dilemma.

There were no such worries on the base. The drugs were treated as a way of relaxing, forgetting about the war and what might happen. Purely recreational. Our group, though we might have been heavy drinkers when off duty, were never guilty of going on patrol stoned, or even partly under the weather. It was a precautionary exercise where mate checked mate, and if there was the slightest inkling that one man could be a danger to himself or the group, he was reported sick and left back on the base. It was as the Major had said, we were like brothers, and as such, wanted to see no one come to any harm.

For six months it worked well for us, with a number of skirmishes with the VC and only a few light casualties suffered. It seemed our company was having a charmed run. The yanks were having a rough time of it, but we seemed to be making inroads with the locals and keeping Charlie at bay — the way we liked it. With only a few months of our tour of duty to go, nobody wanted any problems. Nothing any of us were likely to regret.

The dog stretched and yawned beside me and his paw pushed against my leg in an attempt to wake me. "What?" I asked looking blankly at him, unsure if I had been asleep or only daydreaming. He stood up and turned his head towards the heavens, revealing a row of ominous dark clouds moving slowly towards us. The distant rumble of thunder indicated the storm was not that far away as I packed up and mounted the bike, Red already on the pillion seat behind me. "You hanging on?" I asked, turning to the dog and starting off. This time we followed the tracks that led to the house and other than for the fording of the creek, for which I slowed, the ride was quite uneventful.

I drove directly into the barn and stopped the bike as the first few drops of rain fell. Red jumped off and raced across to the house as though in a hurry to tell Blue what he'd been up to. I had noticed as I drove in that the Mercedes was gone, but wondered if it was only a temporary thing or the Major had gone back to his home. I had barely removed the remaining food from the saddle bag as Rebecca came running into the barn, her hair and clothes slightly damp from the falling rain.

"You got back in time," she cried out, brushing her face and hair and looking back at the rain.

"Only just. Where's the Major?"

"He's gone. At least for a few days. He'll phone when he's coming back. He tried to convince me it wasn't worth my while keeping you on," she said with a grin.

"He's determined," I muttered, walking over and standing beside her, looking out as the rain thundered down on the metal roof, making it almost impossible to hear or talk to each other. "Where are the kids?" I shouted.

She looked at her watch. "The school bus brings them home. I'll go down to the gate in half an hour and wait. How did it go today?"

"All done. The fences will be all right for a bit longer," I replied. I stood close enough beside her to feel the warmth of her body through the damp clothes. "The Major is worried people will talk about you and me, being here together on the property."

She turned her head and looked over at me, her eyes staring into mine. "Are you worried about that?"

The question took me by surprise and I hesitated before answering. "I don't think so. Should I be?"

"People will talk, regardless. A married woman with two children and a young virile stranger staying with them, that should get their tongues wagging, don't you think?" She said it as though she relished the thought of having the gossip mongers go crazy.

"It was one thing the Major was trying to avoid."

"Then it will give him something else to fume about," she answered flippantly.

Her reply surprised me. "Do I take it from that, you don't get on with him all that well?"

"I told you he was a bully. His son is a bully, and I don't want my son growing up in the same vein as that," she answered briefly with no further explanation.

I looked out at the rain as a flash of light cut through the barn followed almost immediately by a clap of thunder which shook everything in the barn. Rebecca jumped and wrapped her arms about me, hugging me tightly. My reaction was to hold her, though not tightly, feeling confused by our conversation and her actions. She showed no sign of releasing her hold, and I must admit the warmth and feeling that flowed between us made me unsure that I wanted to be the one to release my grip.

We stood there for some time, just holding each other and watching the rain, neither of us saying a word, bathing in the warm romantic embrace we found ourselves in. As the rain eased, she let her hold on me loosen and said. "I'd better go for the kids. They'll worry if I'm not there to meet them. Come across for dinner about seven." She released her hold and ran out into the rain, jumped into the truck, and drove off, leaving me standing, watching, confused about what had happened.

I'd hardly spoken to Rebecca over the past day, but the happy family picture she'd painted on that first night appeared to be nothing more than pretense. The truck disappeared down the hill and into the cover of the rain as I finally broke from the spell and moved closer to the open doorway. The rain continued, heavier at times, hammering down on the iron roof, making it virtually impossible to think—and I now had much more to think about.

My first impressions had been that of a loving, happy wife and husband, along with a concerned father-in-law, but perhaps everything was not as it seemed. She'd mentioned the Major was a bully, but now admitted the son was as well. This left me to wonder that all was not well in the marriage and that the husband might not be missed, as I had originally thought. This also made my position at the property even more exposed than I had realised. I had made my mind up after the last romantic debacle that I wanted nothing more to do with women in a serious way. Though brief encounters were not ruled out, I'd given no thought to a married woman with children.

Work was to be my therapy. Something to keep my mind distracted from the effects of war and my body active, working the joints and muscles that had suffered so much trauma. The doctors were pleased with my recovery, though the scars I'd bear for life. It had happened in much the same weather like this. Heavy rain, monsoon weather and perfect for an ambush, concealed amongst the jungle, thick shrub and trees. There was failing light which added to our woes, and when the first gunshots rang out, everyone in the patrol dived for cover.

I shook my head, hoping to drive out the memory, but knew that was impossible and walked back into the barn and looked about for something to do—anything to take my mind off the demons that would surely return if I didn't.

The storm had abated by nightfall, and there was coolness and crispness in the air as I made my way over to the house. I'd seen Rebecca return with the children earlier, but was in no hurry to interrupt her time with the children or preparing the dinner. Besides, I had plenty to tinker about with while I waited, clearing the bench and checking the tools, some of which were rusted from lack of use.

Toby was the first to greet me, opening the door, and taking me through to the dining area where Helen was already seated at the table. "Make yourself comfortable," Rebecca shouted from the kitchen. "Dinner won't be long."

I did as she requested, sitting where I had the night before when the Major was there. Toby sat down and stared at me with his usual suspicious look.

"How long are you going to stay here?" he asked.

"As long as your mother wants me to. There's a lot of work to be done here," I answered truthfully.

"Nothing I can't do," he replied, recalling what his grandfather had told him.

"Do you like my mother?" Helen asked.

I was taken aback by the question and could only wonder what else the children had heard or been discussing. "I think she's very nice," I replied, hoping that would suffice.

"You know she's married to my father?" she continued.

"I've heard that mentioned."

"He's away at the war, but he'll be home soon," she told me.

"As soon as he's won the war," Toby added arrogantly.

I was amused by the way he spoke, as though his father would single-handedly defeat the enemy, but then I wasn't sure what the Major had been telling the boy. "I'm sure it won't be long at all."

"I hope you're hungry," Rebecca said.

She walked in from the kitchen with a bowl full of veggies and stew, placing it on the table. She then took the ladle and scooped out some of the delicious-smelling meal onto the plates of the children and myself before filling hers and sitting down.

"Are we saying, *Grace*?" Toby asked.

"If you want, but Grandfather's not here," Rebecca replied.

Without hesitation, Toby started to eat, prompting everyone at the table to follow suit. The meal was simple but filling, and when we were finished there was nothing left on any plate.

"Time to get ready for bed," Rebecca told the two children, who both unhappily agreed, getting up and leaving the table.

I was surprised when Helen turned to me and said goodnight before leaving the room, the first time she had said much to me at all.

I helped with the clearing up, taking the plates through to the kitchen, this time not facing any protests from Rebecca.

"What were you planning for tomorrow?" she asked as she started to wash the dishes.

"I might have a look at the tractor and some of those implements, if that's all right by you?" I told her, waiting to dry up, tea-towel in hand.

"They haven't gone for quite a while." She looked at the tea-towel. "You don't have to do that. I can do it."

"I've nothing else to do, although I'm out of practice at doing it," I admitted.

"It's something Geoffrey wouldn't do, but if you want to get back in the swing of it, I certainly won't stop you." She grinned and continued washing the dishes.

"Just what did Geoffrey do around here?" I asked casually.

"To be truthful . . . nothing. He believed the wife was responsible for all the household duties, including around the house. He tried his hand at everything, once, and if it didn't appeal to him, that was the end of it. It was left to me, and you can see where that ended up."

"Considering . . . you've done a fairly good job. Life on the land isn't easy. When do you expect him back home? Here, I mean?"

"Who knows? His father will know before me, but I'm in no hurry. We're all better off without him," she said, again leaving me to think all was not as it seemed.

I looked cautiously at her. "I'm a little confused. I thought at first you were . . ."

"For the sake of the children, we seem a happy loving couple, but that's far from the truth, Richard. Geoffrey is like his father—controlling. I seem to have the Major keeping an eye on me even when he's not around, and Geoffrey knows everything that goes on here. I expect a letter from him at any time now telling me to get rid of you."

"If it's that bad, would you rather I went and be done with it?" I asked.

"No! For some reason, I feel *safe* around you, though I'm not sure that's the right word. I need you here." She looked over at me, a look of desperation on her face.

"I don't want to cause any trouble for you and the kids."

"You won't," she replied adamantly.

I wished I could be so sure, but while we were having such an honest tell-all, I casually asked, "Are you into drugs at all?"

She nearly dropped a plate and looked over at me incredulously.

"Do you think I'm high and making all this up?"

"No. What I meant was—"

"I've tried a few things, but not in the past few years. What are you inferring?"

"Nothing. I shouldn't have asked."

"Then why did you?"

"Why?" I felt I was already in trouble and only the depth

44

now would vary. "When I was fixing the fence, I stumbled across a crop of marijuana plants. I wasn't sure if . . . you might have had . . . some involvement with it," I said, floundering over the wording.

"What? A crop? Where? Not on my property." She was clearly aghast at the suggestion.

"I couldn't imagine you'd be involved, but these days growing drugs has become quite a lucrative business."

"Of course, I'm not involved, but what's it doing here? If the police find out, I could go to jail. Who's behind it? My neighbour?" She was so emotional, she started swinging about a china plate, and I was worried she was either going to throw it at me or drop it.

Fear showed in her eyes and I did my best to console her and take the plate from her hand. "I don't know, but the crop is close to harvesting, so whoever is behind it will have to act fairly soon. I'd say by the look of it, whoever they are have been operating for some time without your knowing about it. I doubt that will change. If you can, forget I said anything about it and we'll let matters run their course. That way at least you won't be involved."

"How can I forget what you just said? And I *am* involved. It's being grown on my property. I probably should let the Major know."

"No. Don't say anything to anyone. At least that way it can't be said you know about it if anyone finds out. I'm sorry I told you, but I was worried for you and the kids."

She put the last of the dishes down and wiped her hands. "Thanks for that, but I somehow wish I didn't know. More bloody drama!"

I put the dish down and hung the tea-towel back on the rack, then turned to Rebecca. "Don't worry about it. I'll keep my eye on things. You just go about your normal day and keep smiling."

"That won't be all that easy," she said, her eyes looking soulfully into mine.

I felt like holding her as we had that afternoon and kissing those warm tender lips, but I was still unsure of this woman. I took her hand and held it warmly. "You'll be fine."

She squeezed my hand and gave me a pleading look.

I gagged and coughed. "Thanks for dinner. I should be going."

"Are you sure?" She gave that pleading look again, which I felt had dubious undertones.

"I . . . the kids . . . yes." I blundered over the words as I made my way from the kitchen, nearly falling over myself as I opened the door to the verandah and hurried out, over to the barn . . . and safety.

CHAPTER SIX

I spent an uncomfortable night, tossing and turning, and although I felt I slept little, I remembered the battle in the rain and heat of the jungle and was now faced with this new conflict that was entering my life, here at home. Becoming involved with a married woman would never have crossed my mind when I started this journey, though I still had time to leave. *Go, while the going is easy and get out and move on to a more uncomplicated place in my life.* If I stayed here, I wasn't sure how I would end up, but I wasn't one to run from a damsel in distress, and I felt she was badly in need of help — my help, as no one else seemed to care.

I stayed in the barn that morning, munching on the leftovers from the day before and working on the tractor. I heard the children playing and yelling until Rebecca took them to the school bus before all went quiet. Red had joined me, possibly hoping for another ride on the bike, but waiting patiently, watching as I worked on the engine of the derelict machine.

It seemed like what Rebecca had said was right, that Geoffrey was a tinkerer and knew and cared little about what he had. He had all the equipment and tools to care for and run the farm economically, but wasn't interested. A shame, because the place had the potential to become self-sufficient and profitable with a bit of sweat, tears and know how. The soil was fertile and there was plenty of land for grazing their own cattle if they'd bothered to buy some.

"Let's see what that does," I said to Red moving to the side of the tractor and turning the key, waiting as the glow plug lit before starting the motor. The dog barked as the tractor engine roared into life, sending a cloud of black smoke through the barn as it did. I coughed, the fumes getting into my throat as I waited for the smoke to clear and listened as the engine settled down to a steadier idle. "One for us," I said to the dog, pleased with my success.

"So, you're a mechanic as well," a strong male voice called out.

I looked through the thinning smoke and saw the figure of a uniformed person standing inside the doorway, watching me. Amid the noise and smoke, neither Red nor I had seen or heard him. "As well as what?" I asked.

"Word has it, you're a trouble maker," the voice replied, moving closer.

He was a police officer, the three stripes on the shirt indicating the rank of Sergeant while his uniform looked clean and well fitting. He was a big man, well built with a no-nonsense look on his face.

I moved away from the tractor into the light where I could see him better. "And you are?"

"Sergeant Daley, from the local police. What's your name?" he asked.

He took out a notebook and looked at me as if my face appeared on a wanted poster in his station.

"Richard Scott, but I'm sure you already know that."

"Don't get smart with me. I was told there was some hot-shot making a nuisance of himself out here. I thought I'd better come and check you out before there's any trouble," he said in an authoritative tone.

"Since when has working been a crime?"

"We have quite a few people pass through here saying they are looking for work, but not all are. You find some defence-less woman with a couple of kids and think you're onto a good thing, but around here, we look after our folk. Your type aren't wanted around here," he finished, giving me a veiled warning.

"My type? What type is that?" I asked sarcastically. "It sounds more like the Major talking than some respected police officer," I added. trying hard to keep my temper in check.

"I think you should pack up your gear and hop on that bike and leave before I find you're wanted for something, somewhere else," he warned.

"I'm not wanted for anything. You've no doubt checked up on that already. As I've told the Major, when Rebecca tells me to go, that's when I'll leave. And not before."

"You've been warned," he said putting his notebook back in his pocket, having scribbled nothing down. "Make one wrong move and you'll be behind bars quicker than you can blink. I'll be keeping an eye on you."

Rebecca returned in the truck and parked alongside the police utility and hopped out seeing the Sergeant in the shed and hurried across. "You got it going," she said to me, clearly elated the tractor was idling away. She turned to the Sergeant. "What are you doing here, Tom?"

"Heard you had someone out here supposedly working for you and thought I'd better come and check him out," he replied.

"Well, you can see he's working. So far, he's fixed the fences and now he's got the tractor going. I don't appreciate you snooping about for no good reason, Tom," she told him in a chastising, but friendly way.

"Just doing my job," he told her. "And remember what I told you," he said, turning back to me as he started to walk from the shed.

I didn't answer and watched as he and Rebecca walked out and over to his vehicle. They talked for some time before he got in and drove slowly out, Rebecca watching until he was out of sight before coming back into the shed.

"Did he try to warn you off?" she asked. She seemed offended.

"He mentioned it, but I told him you were the only one that could get rid of me."

"He said that. He thought you were a bit brazen. It was all the Major's doing. Tom's all right. I've known him since we shifted here. He's like a friend of the family. He calls in on occasions to make sure things are good," Rebecca said. "His kids go to school with mine."

"So, I've still got a job?"

Her eyes widened in shock that I'd even asked.

"Of course . . . unless you want to leave?"

I smiled. "No. Not until I've ploughed up a few acres, at least." I walked back to the idling tractor, stepped up to the seat and checked the gears, grating them gently until they dropped into place, then slowly moved the tractor from the shed into the sunshine.

After four hours in the warming sunshine breaking ground I had thought would still be moist after the previous day's rain, I found, in reality, it was quite dry and dusty as the discs cut their way through the soil. Farming had not been my calling, but as the hours wore on, I felt I was doing a respectable job of ploughing a few acres near where Rebecca and the children had set about digging their field of corn by hand. The one thought that hadn't crossed my mind was whether Rebecca had seed for planting, but that was only a minor detail. I felt good with myself as I drove the tractor back to the barn, considering I'd ploughed enough ground and the tractor had proved more reliable than I'd expected.

I stopped the machine and sat back on the seat, daydreaming for a moment.

"You hungry?"

I turned and looked down, surprised I hadn't heard

Rebecca approach.

"Famished." I smiled and hopped down from the tractor and brushed my clothes, not realising how dusty I was.

"I brought some leftovers from last night," she said displaying a plate of hot stew and vegetables. "Do you want to clean up first?"

"Not much point in that. I'll have this and go to the dam and wash my clothes and might even take a dip. It was warm out there," I said, sitting down and taking the plate from her and commencing to eat.

"There'll be another storm later."

I hadn't taken any notice of the sky since I'd returned to inside the barn, so I was unable to see what the weather might be doing. "Are you some sort of weather forecaster?"

"Not likely, but usually when we get one storm like we did yesterday, we can expect a run of them for a few days. I think it's the change of seasons."

"I'll keep it in mind when I go to dry the clothes," I replied between taking mouthfuls of the stew, glad Red was not about to give me that forlorn look of hunger he had with the biscuits.

"Hang your clothes in the shed. It will be safer and dryer." She indicated a line strung across with pegs clipped to it.

I nodded and handed her back the empty plate. "What do you want to plant where I ploughed?"

"I hadn't given it any thought. What do you suggest?"

I may have struggled my way through fixing fences and ploughing, but I had no idea what was needed about the farm or what could be grown for market. "You could contact your local farmer's co-op. They should be able to tell you what would be best. I spoke with a chap called Angus at the local store in town. He seemed a knowledgeable sort, and friendly." *Provided you weren't looking for work.*

"I know him. I'll give him a call and see what he suggests," she said, taking the plate and walking back to the house.

I gathered all my dirty clothes and walked down the hill to the dam, dropping what I was carrying into the shallows and taking a look about before taking off my shirt and shoes and jeans and entering the cool water.

I sat down in the water realising how much dirt I had ingrained in my arms and hair and, taking the soap, began to scrub madly to find the man beneath the dirt. I looked up at the sky remembering what Rebecca had said about the weather, but it was relatively clear and blue. "So much for the forecast," I muttered to myself as I scrubbed my legs and feet before taking the clothes and giving them a wash, then tossing them onto the bank.

"How's the water?"

I turned sharply to see her standing near the water's edge.

That was twice she'd crept up on me without my noticing and I was wondering if I was losing my ability to sense or hear someone approaching. "Wet and soapy," I joked.

"Would you like company?"

"In here?"

"We all used to bathe in there at one time. It was very relaxing," she said, starting to undress.

"Do you think the Major would approve?" I asked, as she removed her blouse and skirt and stepped into the water in only a pair of panties and bra.

She gave me a coy and sexy grin. "Are you likely to tell him?"

"That we were swimming together nearly naked in the dam, or that you were trying to seduce me?" I asked, unsure which.

She smiled mischievously. "Does either bother you?"

"Only if we get found out, but as I'm already the bad boy here, yours would be the only reputation damaged, which was what the Major was trying to avoid," I replied as she edged closer to me.

"Let me worry about the Major," she said as she brushed against me, settling in the water beside me.

"And the children?"

She put her hand on my shoulder and slowly slid it around my neck and pulled me to her.

"They'll never know," she whispered as her lips closed over mine.

It was all I imagined it would be—warm, tender, yet hungry and impatient, and I was sure we both savoured that kiss more than any we'd had before. When we broke apart, our eyes looked clearly into the other's as if asking silently for some response, something to say this should continue . . . but perhaps not here.

"That girl who broke your heart was mad," she whispered, without taking her eyes from mine.

Eleanor was the furthermost person from my mind at that point, but the mention of her name brought back the memory and the thought that I did not want to go through that again, especially not when there were a husband and children involved.

"The war makes strange bedfellows for some people. I don't feel right about this . . . your husband and the kids . . ." I said reluctantly.

"My husband is in bed with the war and, I'm guessing, a lot of women I don't know and certainly don't want to know about. He hasn't touched me in two wonderful years—frustrating, but wonderful years. The children, although they say they miss him, are better off without him. I'm sure if he didn't come back home, they'd barely notice."

"I'm not looking for a partner," I blurted out, trying to make my position clear, though if I had been, Rebecca would have been perfect.

"Neither am I, which makes this excellent." She smiled and

backed away, starting to swim away from me towards the middle of the dam. "Does that make you feel better?"

I wasn't sure how I was feeling. *Numb?* She was taunting me, swimming backstroke, watching for my reaction as she kicked away. I gave chase, like a greyhound after a hare, realising the seduction scene I had imagined had now been turned topsy-turvy with me chasing after her. It took only a few strokes to catch up before I was swimming alongside her, looking into those dark eyes and avoiding the occasional splash as her hands broke the surface of the water. "What is it you want from me?" I asked, thinking the question was stupid, but I felt confused and needed to hear what she had to say.

"Would sex be too much to ask? Companionship? Someone to hold me when I need it? Talk intimately to? I need you, Richard, I can't be any more direct than that," she added as she stopped swimming and turned to me, treading water effortlessly.

It was the most candid a woman had been with me for some time, including Eleanor. She'd never been that direct with me, leaving me to make the moves and simply going with it. In Saigon, the women were that direct and more, but there was always the money side, so it was expected. Now, here was a woman, a beautiful woman, offering me all I could have had with Eleanor and more, with no recriminations, no guilt, no limitations, and still I was hesitant. What more could a man want?

I wasn't sure what to say as thinking of Eleanor brought back bitter memories.

I'd fallen for her head over heels and she had those same feeling for me — so she said. I'd started my building business and it was going great and things were booming. She moved in with me to my rented house and together we were saving like mad to buy that perfect block of land, so I could build that perfect house for us both, and then we were planning the perfect wedding followed by the perfect life after. Then came the call-up papers, throwing everything including our lives and dreams into disarray.

"I'm flattered. I . . ." I was speechless, not sure what else to say.

"Don't be. It's purely a matter of need — *my* need." She grinned, closing her arms around my neck as her lips once again found mine, warmly and tenderly. We had both been treading water, but as the kiss became more intense — passionate, I felt my body start to sink only to touch a gravel bottom with her legs wrapped around mine.

"It's not as deep as I thought," I whispered when our lips parted.

"Deep enough," she whispered back. "Toby nearly drowned in here."

"How? When?"

"When Geoffrey was last home. He threw him in and told him to swim to shore. Toby panicked, but Geoffrey refused to help. I ended up diving in and helping the boy out. He's never been back in the water since, and Geoffrey hasn't been home. It's been peaceful without him," she said distastefully.

"You don't love him anymore?" It was a question that had been troubling me, and now with his wife clinging to me seductively, it seemed a good time to ask.

"I did at the start. He seemed to be the perfect husband and father, but as time went on, he turned out to be just like his father — a bully and wife . . ." She went silent for a moment resting her face against mine.

"He beat you?"

"Occasionally . . . but never in front of the children," she added, as though that made it all right.

"What about Toby and Helen?"

"They had their fair share of hidings, some deserved, but most just so he could inject fear into them . . . have them obey him."

"And yet you stayed with him?" I shook my head.

"I thought about leaving a number of times, but where could I go with virtually no money and two children? Then he went into the army and that was a blessing, even more so when he was sent to Vietnam. I had no reason to go after that. There was only the Major, and although he likes to order me around and be in control, he's never attempted to be forceful with me. It's usually just threats."

As we spoke, I had been slowly moving towards the shore, my feet feeling their way over the sandy and graveled bottom of the dam, while her legs had remained entwined about me and her body hard against mine, causing me some discomfort and feelings I was enjoying the longer we stayed as we were. She had told me everything I thought there was to tell about her life with Geoffrey and the farm, holding back little about the way she felt about him and the Major, filling in the gaps on the snippets she had already spoken to me about.

"We should get out," I said quietly to her as our bodies were well out of the water and her legs were still wrapped about me in some erotic, but pleasant hold.

"Before it rains and we both get wet?" she asked.

I thought she was joking until I looked about at the blackening sky and realised she'd been right in her forecast of the weather. "Where did that come from?" I was surprised by the sudden change in the colour of the sky and gently let her slide from me into the water.

CHAPTER SEVEN

It was amazing how quickly the conditions changed. By the time we'd gathered our clothes and those that I'd washed, the sky had turned to a blackish-green and the wind was blowing in cool hard gusts. Without dressing, we hurried up the hill to the barn, rushing inside as the wind picked up and rain started to fall. I emptied my arms of the clothes I'd washed and closed the doors as best I could, chaining them together since the wind caused them to flap and bang against each other. Another job I would have to get onto when the weather cleared.

"Do you want to race across to the house?" I asked, thinking Rebecca might feel more secure inside her home.

"No," she answered coming to me and holding me tightly. By now, the wind had picked up with forceful gusts that shook the barn as they hit, and the rain—no, hail—began pounding on the roof, making it impossible to hear one speak.

I motioned to my bed, the divan where I slept, and Rebecca went willingly, sliding between the sheets and covering herself with the blanket as I crawled in beside her, feeling the warmth of her body against mine, though our clothes, or what we were wearing, were still damp. We hugged and kissed under the bedclothes as the sound of the afternoon storm rumbled outside. Flashes of light followed by loud crashes of thunder only increased the volatility of the situation as Rebecca displayed her fear of nature's wrath. Her arms held me tightly at every flash or crash and her legs intertwined with mine, ensuring nothing would separate us beneath the bedclothes.

It was some time after we had become comfortable in our world beneath the blanket that one of us, I'm not sure if it was Rebecca or myself, began to explore the other, though it might have been mutual. Our lips had barely parted for the whole time, but in the confines of such a small area and with the closeness of our bodies, mine was behaving as any virile man's might and making it rather uncomfortable for us both. My hand dropped to try to alleviate the pressure that was being pressed against her by my engorged penis, constricted by the wet underpants I was wearing.

Her thought must have been similar, as our hands met while I was attempting to slide the wet pants over my embarrassment. Rebecca helped, although I felt uncomfortable, fumbling, attempting to get them off.

Rebecca laughed aloud. "It would have been easier if we'd undressed before we got in."

Easy to say in retrospect, and though we wore little, the wet underwear was proving to be a hassle—at least mine was. There was a frantic amount of movement under the blanket, arms and legs moving in different directions, along with a number of grunts and groans as we bumped heads and tangled feet in clothing, and for a moment daylight crept in giving us both a chance to see what we were doing.

The thoughts of the storm, wind, and rain had been erased in our haste to undress what little we had and as the underpants and panties were kicked out of the end of the divan, we both settled warmly against each other again. Again, the kissing became passionate, heated as our bodies moved for position. I was never sure at first what this woman liked or how she liked it, but I moved to the position that I guessed was more common, yet less exciting and waited for some reaction from Rebecca before continuing.

"Is there something wrong?" she asked, as I stopped,

poised to enter.

"Condoms are in the saddle bag."

"You don't need them."

She thrust her hips upwards in anticipation, without waiting for a response. I obliged.

She let out a slight whimper, her face giving a satisfied look as I dropped gently down, feeling the warmth and moistness within her. With her eyes closed, her lips again sought out mine, our tongues teasing each other as I moved slowly over her. Gently, gently, taking my time, feeling this woman had missed out on so much and deserved so much more. The time was our own, and with thanks to the storm, she had achieved what she set out to do and I had willingly accommodated her needs.

Then why did I feel there was something wrong?

I lifted my head suddenly, the blanket sliding off, allowing us both to see daylight and that the storm had actually blown itself out.

"What's wrong?" Rebecca asked, unnerved by my sudden movement.

"The time. The storm's over. What about the kids?"

I moved my body and detached myself, hurrying from the divan and checking my watch. "It's after four."

"Blast!" she cried swinging her legs over the edge of the divan and looking about for her clothes. "The bus will be waiting. I didn't think."

She was flustered, searching the bed, then the floor. I gathered her dress and blouse and tossed them to her.

"I'll leave the rest," she said struggling into the blouse and hurriedly slipping on the dress. "The kids won't notice. Can you clean up?"

"Sorry to end it like that."

"No. Don't be. I was in another world. I should have known."

She sounded apologetic, yet disappointed, and I had to agree it was not the best ending we could have achieved, but now the ice was broken. The next time, if there was to be a next time, we would prepare more carefully.

"Thanks. I'll get the kids. Come over about seven for dinner," she said as she hurried out of the barn and across to the utility and quickly drove off.

I looked at the divan and wished I kept my mind on the job, but Rebecca felt bad enough. I found my underpants and sat down to put them on, finding her panties under the blanket when I picked that up and set about remaking the bed. Her bra was tangled up and fell out as I shook the blanket so I put that aside with the panties so she could collect them at another time.

I hung out what clothes I'd washed, feeling the cool draught that penetrated the barn through all the gaps and cracks would soon dry them. After that, I dressed in my old clothes and wandered about looking for something to do.

It was dark as I walked across to the house, hoping Rebecca had made amends with the children after running late to collect them and caught up with any of the household chores she would normally have had done before they arrived home from school. My customary knock on the door was answered by Helen, who informed me immediately that *mummy hasn't got the dinner ready yet, but you can come in anyway.* She led me through to the dining table and beckoned me to sit in my usual chair as she resumed her seat next to her brother. Red came over and sniffed at me, then went back and sat with Blue. I found out both dogs had been locked inside, since neither liked storms.

"Is that you, Richard?" Rebecca called from the kitchen.

"Yes," I replied. "Do you need a hand?"

She came to the doorway and smiled. "No. It's nearly

ready. That storm this afternoon put me all behind. It won't be long." She turned and headed back to the kitchen.

"Mum doesn't like storms," Toby said, sitting patiently. "What did you do today?"

"A bit of ploughing and some washing."

"In the rain?" Helen queried.

"No, before it started, though I did get wet."

"A bit of water never hurt anyone," Toby recited as though the phrase was commonly used.

"You didn't get wet either?" I asked.

"We were on the bus," Toby replied.

"And mummy was late coming to get us. The bus driver was cross," Helen chimed in.

"I hope she didn't get into trouble," I said.

Rebecca came through the doorway holding onto two plates which she put in front of the children.

"Who's in trouble?" she asked, looking from me to the children.

"The children were saying the bus driver was angry you were late picking them up," I said as convincingly as possible.

"Fred's all right. He understands I don't like storms all that much." She smiled.

"But the storm was over," Toby insisted.

Rebecca looked at her son. "I told you, water got in the engine of the truck and I had trouble starting it. Ask Richard."

Toby looked my way, sceptical and hesitant to ask, if what his mum was saying was true.

"That's right," I replied, taking Rebecca's lead. "There was water everywhere."

"You'll have to show me what to do so I can help next time it happens," he said, then continued eating.

I looked across at Rebecca and smiled, hoping we had weathered the last of that storm.

After dinner, Rebecca set about putting the children to bed and I started the clearing of the table.

"Leave that. I'll do it," she said coming into the kitchen and taking my hand. "You've done enough today. Perhaps you should go to the barn and rest."

I smiled. I'd done nothing really. I'd hardly exerted myself. "Are you sure? I don't mind helping."

"I appreciate all you've done. Now, go and rest." She led me from the kitchen to the verandah where she turned and gave me a warm kiss. "I'd prefer you stayed here with me, but for the sake of the children . . ."

"That's fine. I'll see you in the morning." I gave her a brisk kiss on the cheek and hurried down the stairs, Red joining me as I went across to the barn.

The lantern cast a dull glow and ghostly shadows through the barn as I sat down on the divan and commenced to undress, removing my shoes and socks and shirt before thinking about the events of the day, and mainly Rebecca. She was certainly a woman with needs, and I felt sorry for her meeting up with a ruffian like Geoffrey, although she admitted they were happy at first until he showed his real colours. How does a woman let a man push and belt her around like that? Even her children. The man was . . . I was angry just thinking about it. Rebecca was beautiful and everything a man could want. And the children, they seemed normal and happy. What was wrong with the man?

I stood up and let the pants slide down my legs and sat down again to remove them properly, leaving me sitting in my underpants. The same pair that had been wet and a source of annoyance during the afternoon frolic with Rebecca. I stood up again and went to the lantern and turned it down, extinguishing the flame, the only light now coming from the stars through the open doors. Red whimpered and curled up on his mat near the divan as I walked back, removed the undies and lifted the blanket and settled on the divan. I wasn't sure what tomorrow would bring, but I was happy to take one day at a time, especially with a woman like Rebecca.

I heard Red give a low growl before I felt a warm hand gently touch my shoulder.

"Move over," Rebecca whispered.

"What are you doing here?" I asked, surprised by her action, moving my body over to accommodate her.

"We've some unfinished business."

She grinned, tossing aside her housecoat and kissing me, pushing me back until her body was firmly planted on the divan and hard against mine.

"What about the children?"

"They're both asleep. They are early risers, though, so make sure if I go to sleep, you get me up early."

"You're staying the night?"

She frowned, looking hurt. "You don't want me to?"

"Of course, I do. It was just . . ." It was not the time for conversation. Rebecca's intentions were clear, and who was I to argue? There was no tangling of clothes as there were none and the clash of naked bodies warmly against each other was the catalyst which had her moaning and groaning as I continued where I had so hastily left off earlier that day. This time there was no storm or children to terminate the act between us, only the desire to please each other.

My hand traced the outline of her body, feeling the fullness and roundness of her breasts and the hardened nipples that sat so blatantly firm and upright, awaiting the sensual touch of my lips. The slim waist which blossomed to the hips and thighs now clinging to me, moving in gentle harmony with me, enjoying the movement, the thrusting and withdrawal. Wanting more.

It seemed I had taken little time to get to know Rebecca. Even in the dam that afternoon, I had barely noticed her figure, though we had talked and frolicked, and later on the divan under the blanket. Until then, it had always been her face, that pleasant smile which had captivated me, but now there was more, so much more. Although the darkness obstructed my ability to see, I had formed a mental picture, connecting the face to the body in my mind, through the gentle touch of my hands.

A low moan from her lips brought me back from my wandering and had me concentrate again on my objective. "I'm close," she whispered, her teeth gently nipping at the lobe of my ear.

I felt her gasp, pant, as her legs tightened about me before she let out a long low muffled cry. Her body convulsed with mine, attempting to keep with her as she appeared to writhe in ecstasy, then settle, her heart thumping against me as her breathing sounded as erratic as mine was at that moment.

"Oh, God . . . I needed that." She gasped, opening her eyes and looking up at me. "Did you?"

"You did say there was no need for a condom?"

She grinned. "You're safe. Hold me."

She released me from the hold her legs had on me and we cuddled together for some time, neither of us saying a word, just enjoying the warmth we had created between us. We were both sweaty, but that didn't matter. The body odour between us was not unpleasant, though the aroma of ravenous sex did hang low around the divan.

Red must have noticed some untamed air about. He became unsettled on his mat, then got up to investigate.

The silence was broken when Rebecca let out a scream and kicked her legs, bringing them up, nearly causing me a painful injury. "What's wrong?" I yelled, starting to get off the divan.

"Something . . ." She started to laugh.

I looked at her, unsure what was happening.

"It was Red," she said, looking at the end of the divan where Red was sitting, watching us. "Something licked and nuzzled my foot. I got a fright and reacted. I'm sorry." She laughed again.

"Back to bed, Red," I ordered the dog, who had no idea of the fuss he'd caused and so sauntered back to his mat.

I slid back under the blanket giving myself a rub in a place that had connected with Rebecca's knees, but her hands were there to help and offer some compassion. It was the start of another arduous incursion which lasted for most of the night.

CHAPTER EIGHT

Dawn was breaking when I awoke. Rebecca was lying against me, my arm wrapped around her, her breathing quiet and regular, a change to what it had been at different times during the night. I lifted the blanket to get a better look at the body I had feasted on for most of the night, but thought better of exploring further as time did not permit. I gave her a shake of the shoulder as I kissed her gently on the lips and listened as she murmured a few words and slowly opened her eyes.

"What?"

"Time to get up—it's daylight."

"Oh. Damn." She struggled to sit up and look out of the barn doors at the lightening day. "I thought we might . . . damn." She slid over me, her lips connecting with mine for a short time. "If you gotta go . . ." She looked about and picked up her housecoat from where she'd tossed it and struggled into it. "Will you come for breakfast?"

"Perhaps after the children have gone to school. I don't want to intrude too much."

"You're not intruding." She rubbed her hair. "How do I look?"

"Like someone who's had sex all night . . . and enjoyed it."

"Good. That's how I feel. Gotta go," she said and hurried out of the barn, Red following her, possibly hoping for some breakfast, or wanting to tell Blue all about what he'd seen and heard in the barn that night.

I lay on the divan thinking about the night before, in no

hurry to get up or think about what I might do that day. From the way the light had brightened in the doorway, I guessed it was going to be sunny, but would have to query Rebecca as to whether it was likely to storm again later. I was hopeful. After some time, I heard children talking and laughing and one of the dogs barking as the utility start up, then all went quiet again. There was no telling how much sleep we'd both had as we rested between bouts, sometimes talking, but mostly gathering our strength for the next session.

I sat up, dropping my legs over the edge of the divan, and looking about for my clothes. Once dressed, I sat back and waited until I heard the utility return before going to the entrance of the barn and looking across as Rebecca hopped out gingerly from the cab. She looked over and saw me. "Would you like some breakfast now?" she called out.

I nodded, walked over to her and gave her a kiss. "What did you have in mind?"

I felt her body shudder slightly as she gave me a sexy grin. "I think food. You need to keep your strength up."

"You're the boss," I said, giving her a gentle squeeze and another kiss.

"After last night, I wonder," she muttered, taking my hand and leading me into the house. The two dogs barked as we entered, but when they saw who it was, settled back.

"Can we expect another storm today?" I asked, sitting down in my usual seat as she went through to the kitchen.

"That depends."

"On what?"

"What are you doing today?"

"What's that have to do with it?"

She came from the kitchen carrying two cups of tea and put them down before sitting down beside me. "I thought you might need a rest after last night." There was toast on a plate on the table which she pulled across. "It's fresh but cold, and there's jam."

"What does last night have to do with the weather?" I asked, slightly confused.

She giggled. "Sorry. I misunderstood what you meant. It's been so long since . . . there's a good chance we'll get another storm today. Thunder and lightning, and . . ."

She reached over and draped her arms around my neck and kissed me passionately. She drew back as if to catch her breath. "And I really can't wait."

She clung to me, kissing my face and neck, her hands dropping to unbutton my shirt.

I was overcome but worried if things might be happening too rapidly, too recklessly. I put my hands on her shoulders and pushed her back gently and looked into her eyes. "Rebecca, as much as I want you, you don't think we're rushing this a bit? Last night was perfect, but if we overdo this, someone will notice something is going on — the children, the Major or . . ."

"Damn!" she cursed, her face turning from cheerful to sad. "I had a phone call this morning from the Major. He's coming up for the weekend. Apparently, the men will be down in the next day or so to round up the cattle and take them to market."

"So, we can't get around acting like this, can we?"

"Not while they're here, but the Major is only here for the weekend. And those men . . . I never see them anyway." She shrugged. "They go bush and round up what they can, then leave."

"They don't come here to the house?"

"No. Never."

"Then how do you know they're here? How many men usually come?" I asked. I was bewildered that this woman knew nothing about what was going on under her very nose.

"They use the main entry, then veer off near the creek and

go bush. You can see the truck ruts where they come and go. As for how many men, I've never seen them. Maybe the Major might know."

"So, things will be busy around here for a week or so?" I asked, thinking about what she said.

She shook her head. "It won't seem any different. I never know they're there."

"You haven't forgotten about our little plantation problem?"

"That?" Her mouth agape. "You don't think they have something to do with it?"

"I can't be sure about anything around here, but I'm sure as hell going to be taking a closer look at things when they arrive."

"Should I say something to the Major?"

"No. Say nothing to anyone. It's a secret we'll share. No one else will know."

"Well, what about today, now?" she asked. She wrapped her arms about my neck again, her face drawing closer to mine.

Quietly, I cursed the Major, the marijuana, and my inquisitive streak for distracting me. "How would you feel about a picnic?"

I wasn't sure by the look on her face whether what I was suggesting was a letdown or what she was hoping for, though the smile returned. "That sounds wonderful. Where?"

"You pack a lunch and I'll sort out the rest." I gave her a kiss and she returned it with passion, before getting up and going through to the kitchen.

"I'll be back in half an hour," I called out as I left, leaving the two dogs inside with her. I checked the bike and remembered the place along the creek not far from the hut which seemed ideal for a quiet and relaxing picnic. I knew that there was no work going to be done that day, but then, when you're out to lunch with the boss, who's likely to complain?

I wheeled the bike across the ground to the house and knocked on the door, sending the dogs into a frenzy inside. Rebecca answered shortly after, dressed in shorts and singlet top, with a basket and rug in one hand. "I'm ready," she said cheerfully.

She passed me the basket and rug and closed the door, but not before telling the dogs to behave.

She followed me to the bike and looked at it sceptically. "You expect me to sit on that and hang on to this?"

"No. I'll tie the basket and rug on the back here and I expect you to sit and hang onto me," I told her, seeing she was still apprehensive.

She smirked. "How do I know you're a good driver?"

"You didn't complain last night," I replied boldly. "Besides, if Red can stay on there without holding on, I'm sure you'll manage it."

"I think you're being a bit cheeky," she joshed.

I tied on the basket and rug and helped her straddle the bike before hopping on and starting the engine. "Put your arms around me and hold on." I felt her grip me tightly and slowly started off, letting her get accustomed to the bike.

She leaned her head against mine. "Where are you taking me?"

"Somewhere nice, where you can have a bit of freedom," I told her, increasing the speed. We travelled past the dam and continued to follow the flow of water as it twisted and turned through the hills and valleys of the property.

"That sounds exciting," she replied. "I've never been here before. Is there much more property than this?"

"Sometime when we have nothing to do and all day to do it in, I'll take you all around and you can have a decent look at your place." I drove on, the split-post cattle yard coming into view, and I told Rebecca what they were before she asked.

As the creek widened out and the metal shed came into view, I slowed the bike and stopped.

"Are we here?" She looked about. "What's that shed?"

"I thought I might show you what's going on on your property while we're having a little R. & R. The shed's where they keep some of their tools for harvesting the crop."

"I don't see any plantation of marijuana."

"It's in amongst the trees behind the shed."

"Can I see?"

"Let's get settled here first. The crop's going nowhere—at least not today," I said, getting off the bike and helping Rebecca off.

"It's nice here, grassy with shade trees and the water. Can we swim?"

"I don't see why not. The water's clear." I undid the basket and took the rug and spread it over the grass, placing the basket in the middle. There was a splash behind me and I turned and saw Rebecca had taken advantage of the water on a day that was warming up steadily.

I stood up and watched as she broke the water and floated on her back grinning at me. "Come in. The water's lovely," she shouted, taunting me with her naked body. It was an invitation I readily accepted, stripping off my clothes and diving in after her, coming to the surface beside her. "This is as good as the dam."

"But deeper," I told her after resurfacing, letting my body sink down until I touched the bottom well below the surface.

"Can we go look at the crop now?" she asked, as we both tread water, looking over at the shed at the same time.

"Like this?" I asked, indicating we were both naked.

"Why? There's no one about."

I looked about knowing she was right, but the thought of investigating the crop and shed again in the nude didn't actually appeal to me. Besides, I was having trouble controlling my feelings, just being with Rebecca as we were. "Might it not be better to go back and have something to eat and get dressed, then have a look?"

"That won't leave much time for anything else."

She grinned with that sexy grin she had, but I knew exactly what she meant.

"I suppose if we hurry, we can still have time for the other," I agreed. I started to swim towards the shed, closely followed by Rebecca.

I climbed out of the water ahead of her trying to hide my feelings with my hands. I knew that would be impossible as I was continually thinking about spending more time with Rebecca, and that didn't help matters.

She reached me and instantly saw my dilemma and smiled. "Why didn't you say you'd rather be . . ."

"It can wait," I said hurriedly. "Let's have a look and we can go back and . . ." I reached the shed and opened the door and looked in. Nothing had changed or been moved and I waited as Rebecca moved beside me, purposely rubbing her body against mine just to see me squirm.

"So, where's the crop?" she asked seeing nothing of interest inside the shed.

I was beginning to think I'd done the wrong thing bringing her here, as her only interest appeared to be in the marijuana. "There's a track behind the shed," I said closing the door and walking around to the track and into the trees with her. The thought of being so close to this beautiful naked woman was driving me insane, and I felt sure she knew I was suffering.

Brushing branches and tall growing weeds away from my body helped take my mind off Rebecca, although she complained that some were scratching her and making her itch as we went through to the crop. I stopped when we reached the outskirts and waited as she caught up. "Here's the money spinner you know nothing about." I spread my arm as though introducing a star to the audience.

She looked surprised. "I didn't think it grew this big," she said, gazing at the size of the plants. "What's the strange smell?"

"The plants are ready for harvesting. Some are flowering. Oh, and watch out for the sap flowing on the stems. It's tacky," I told her hoping her interest was satisfied and we could return to other things.

"It looks nothing like what I used to smoke," she said looking closely at the plants.

"There's a bit to be done before you get to that stage," I suggested.

"Could we take some with us?"

"No. You don't want to alert anyone that someone's been here." I grabbed her arm before it reached an overhanging leaf. I pulled her around to face me and as I did, pushed her back against the base of a large gum tree.

"What are you doing?" she asked in a startled voice, but realized and grinned.

"What do you think?" I asked before kissing her on the lips, preventing her from answering. There was a muffled groan as she lifted her legs about my hips and held me tightly. I pushed and lifted, her body moving with mine against the smooth bark of the tree.

"Oh," she moaned. "Why didn't you say you—"

"I thought that was plainly obvious while we were in the water."

"I just wanted to see—"

"You've seen it now. Let's not waste any more time." I pushed, producing another series of moans and groans from her lips, but not of agony, only pleasure.

It seemed pure animal lust, the two of us madly having sex where we stood, amongst the trees and marijuana plants, alone in the wilderness of a property Rebecca owned, but knew nothing about.

CHAPTER NINE

The rest of that day was spent openly enjoying ourselves. Not even with Eleanor had I indulged in such gluttonous sex, though in fairness to Rebecca, it might have been a more mundane and loving afternoon if she hadn't had such an insatiable appetite. What I had started amongst the plants and trees she merely continued in the open, displaying her wantonness and willingness to accept what any woman starved of love and sex would eagerly respond to.

I myself felt no sorrow or sympathy for her husband, Geoffrey, taking this woman for granted while indulging himself in the good life a thousand miles away. He might have been on a tour of duty for his country, but his duty also lay at home with Rebecca and his children, though he saw that differently.

As the day wore on and at times, we lay sated, recovering, my mind wandered back to those days I had left behind, yet I knew would never leave me.

The four bushrangers, we called ourselves, Wylie, Wayne, Conner, and me. We met at basic training and became inseparable – all the way to Vietnam. We bunked together, went on patrol together and when time permitted, got rotten drunk together. But leave was the time I best remembered . . . whether it was Vung Tau, Saigon, or better, five days in Hong Kong or Singapore, we did our best to forget there was a war going on in that neck of the woods.

I was the rock, the one they depended on to keep them out of too much trouble, since I had made my intentions clear that I was staying true to Eleanor and wouldn't be indulging in any of the escapades they would get up to with the local women. That didn't stop us all getting drunk and into fights, but it did give them a certain amount of security to know someone was watching their back.

We actually found it better and safer in Hong Kong, exhausting ourselves visiting the clubs and bars, waking up at times in some unknown godforsaken place after a heavy night, usually with one or two women one of the boys had picked up along the way. It was all good fun and helped relieve the pressure and stress that was ever present back at camp — back at the war.

Wylie was going to be my best man at my wedding when we returned, and Wayne and Conner had made it plain they would be there, invited or not, just to see the woman who was crazy enough to want me for a husband. They loved to rib me about Eleanor, but I didn't mind — at least I had something to look forward to when we arrived home. They were the good times.

After a cleansing swim, it was decided enough was enough and we packed up the rug and basket after what had been a most enjoyable day. The weather had contained itself, with no sign of a storm, and yet the day had been quite warm, as both our bodies showed by the blush colour or our skin in places rarely exposed to its rays. There was no rush to get back as we had kept an eye on the time. Rebecca didn't want another late episode of collecting the children and casting suspicion on us both.

I drove the bike into the barn and helped Rebecca off, giving her a passionate kiss, yet not wanting to start things afresh. I could tell by the look she gave she was thinking about it, but the mention of the children quashed any further thoughts about that. As she hurried back to the house to let the dogs out and clean up, I went and stretched out on the divan. Sleep would come easy tonight, I thought to myself.

I heard the utility start up and drive off and smiled, thinking if Toby asked tonight what I'd been doing all day, how I would answer. I looked about and thought perhaps I should get up and clean up inside the barn. At least, I could answer truthfully about that. Not long after, as I moved things about and cleared extra space around my small living quarters, I heard the utility return and the sound of talking and laughter which usually followed. What I wasn't prepared for was the hum of a second vehicle as it pulled in behind the utility. I looked out to see the Major stepping from his vehicle and looking over towards the barn.

After a short conversation with Rebecca and the children, he strode towards the barn. I busied myself, guessing that he had come to resume his attack on me after checking through my files.

"You're still here," he bellowed as he walked in, as though hoping I wouldn't be.

"For as long as she needs me," I responded, stopping what I was doing and staring him down.

He grunted as though dissatisfied with the remark. "I've spoken with Geoffrey. He doesn't want you here. He wants you to leave."

"I don't work for him. I work for Rebecca."

Again, he gave a dissatisfied grunt, taking out a cigar and biting at the end before gripping it with his teeth and lighting it. "I checked up on you," he said.

He was eyeing me off as if he'd found out something that I knew nothing about.

"So?" I answered uncaringly.

His voice mellowed slightly. "You had a rough time up there, but you handled yourself pretty well." He blew a cloud of smoke from his mouth and nose while waiting for another response.

I waited.

"I've spoken to a friend of mine who could use someone like you."

"Doing what?"

He shrugged. "Odd-job man. A bit of this and that, but the pay is excellent."

"When I'm finished here, I might be interested," I remarked.

"Finish up and you can start tomorrow."

"There's too much to do. I won't let Rebecca down," I told him doggedly.

"I'm trying to be nice about this, boy. You either start to toe the line and do as I ask, or things are going to start to get very rough for you," he growled, smoke belching from his mouth and nose.

"I don't take too kindly to being threatened," I warned.

"Then we're even. I don't like being disobeyed," he growled, smoke again belching from his mouth.

"I've heard that about you and your son. I'm not in the army now, so . . ." I was going to tell him to *bugger off,* but let it slide.

"Before I'm finished with you, you might wish you still were," he retorted.

He stared at me, puffing on his cigar. If he had been about my age, I'd have been tempted to take a swipe at him, and I think he knew that, stepping back cautiously, stopping when he was well out of reach.

"While we're being so open with each other, what do you know about the marijuana crop growing on the property?" I had said to Rebecca to say nothing to him, but I was tired of the cat and mouse game we were playing and thought I'd bring it to a head—at least find out if he knew about it.

The Major stopped puffing on the cigar for a moment, a scowl appearing on his face. "What crop? What are you talking about?" he asked in all seriousness.

"The crop that's ready for harvest, growing in the scrub towards the back of the property." For a moment, his facial features showed concern and had me thinking he actually knew nothing about it until a faint smile curled about his lips and he started puffing on the cigar again.

"There is no crop. You don't know what you're talking about," he said defiantly, looking at me as though I was hallucinating.

"You had that copper Daley come out to warn me off the other day. I nearly said something to him about it, and now I'm sorry I didn't."

The colour drained slightly from his face and he became pensive once again. "You'd be a bloody fool if you did."

"Why is that? Rebecca's not involved—so she says."

"You've told her about it?" This time the cigar nearly dropped from his mouth. "How stupid are you, boy? Do you know what trouble she can get into if the police find that crop here, on the property?"

"That's why I'm giving you time to remove it all and never plant another crop. You asked me how stupid I am. What were you going to do or tell the kids if she'd been sent to jail for some scheme you've concocted?" I raised my voice on equal terms with his.

"It would never have come to that. We had all the bases covered."

"You and Charlie, or you and your son? Or the three of you?" I queried, knowing that was one question he'd refuse to answer.

"You know too much—too much for your own good. And now you've opened your mouth to Rebecca." He shook his head. "How stupid are you?" he repeated.

"She'll say nothing, but this is the last time. Take the crop and get off the property. Next time you come here, it will be to see Rebecca and the kids, nothing more." I gave him an ultimatum I didn't expect him to abide by.

"You can't tell me what to do, boy. I run this property the way I want, not what you or . . ."

It was no good threatening me, and I felt he realised that.

"You've run this property down, endangered your daughter-in-law and the children doing what you've done. You should be ashamed of yourself, though I found those in authority rarely take responsibility for their mistakes, but are always eager for the accolades when things go right." I was on a roll, and he didn't like it.

The Major spat out his cigar, his face red with anger. "You're overstepping the mark, boy." He started walking backwards, intending to leave. "You don't know who you're dealing with. Telling me what to do," he grumbled, glaring at me before finally turning around and went outside. "Watch your back!"

The barn suddenly went quiet as I stood alone, my fists clenched and my temper not yet satisfied. I'd mixed the war I'd returned from with the war that was developing here. A war I had created through injustice. I'd seen it all before, the men who were dead or wounded, forgotten, while the officers who were nowhere to be seen picked up the medals and accolades. It was no wonder there was a growing discontent between the conscripts, enlisted men and officers. I wondered how the Major had made his way through the ranks, and more so, whether he had ever seen or been in action.

I took a few deep breaths and calmed myself.

Walking to the entrance of the barn, I looked across at the house and wondered what the Major was telling Rebecca, or if my outburst would make it impossible for her not to buckle under the pressure the Major was no doubt exerting on her. I was here if she needed me, I knew she knew that, but she was strong-willed. I'd found that out in just a few days and felt she would resist the overbearing braggart. Just how sociable things might be at dinner was yet to be seen.

CHAPTER TEN

The dinner had been just like the other dinners when the Major was there. He said very little to me, and it was obvious from the way Rebecca and the children behaved, he had said nothing of our spat in the barn earlier, which in some ways surprised me. Had it not been for the occasional glare I received from him, I might have thought it was all but forgotten, which in some way irritated me, and I excused myself before dinner was over and returned to the barn. Red must have sensed something was up, as he returned with me and settled on his mat, watching me as I prepared for an uncomfortable night on the divan. I was still annoyed with myself for letting my temper get the better of me.

I extinguished the lamplight and crawled under the blanket, wishing Rebecca was there to accompany me and rid me of what was troubling me. Night lights ghosted at the entrance of the barn, disappearing as clouds drifted over, dousing the barn in darkness. Red tossed and turned nearly as much as I was, wondering if I'd been too outspoken to the Major or not saying enough. Red growled and I told him to be quiet and pulled the blanket up over my head, willing myself to sleep.

It never worked in camp and it didn't work here, although conditions were completely different. It seemed in camp, we never slept, and if we did, it was only temporary, waiting for the morning bugle call or the sound of gunfire to rouse you from your slumber. Here, there was only quiet and the intermittent growl and snore from Red as we both tossed and turned.

"Move over," Rebecca whispered and, for a moment I wasn't sure if I was dreaming or awake.

I turned, pulling the blanket down and looked up at her. I moved over, lifting the blanket and allowing her to slide in beside me. "What are you doing here?"

She lay down and cuddled against me. "Everyone's asleep at the house. What happened with the Major?"

This woman was worse than me. It seemed she thrived on danger.

"What did he tell *you?*"

"Nothing. That's why I guessed something *did* happen when you left dinner early. What did he say?" she asked.

Her lips were a breath away from mine, not allowing me to answer as they warmly enclosed on my own.

It was some of what I needed to rid me of my anger, but not all. Our lips parted.

"We had a rowdy exchange of words, about the marijuana crop. I told him you knew about it."

"What did he say?" she asked again.

"Told me I was a bloody fool for telling you and I told *him* to get it off the property or else."

"Or else what?"

"It didn't really get to that." It might have if I'd had more time.

"That's why he made the call to Charlie," she mused.

"He rang Charlie? What for?"

"I couldn't hear the conversation, but I guessed something was wrong when he went quiet. Did he threaten you?"

"There was a sort of mutual agreement. We threatened each other." I grinned.

"You know he doesn't like to be told what to do."

"Especially not by workers or women, I gather." She cuddled closer. "You shouldn't be here. What happens if the

Major or the children wake up?"

"They won't," she insisted, moving her body over me and settling in a position which satisfied us both, before starting a gentle rocking motion.

"What's this Charlie fellow like?" I asked quietly, feeling the last of my anger subside and drift away with her movements.

"I've never met him," she answered and groaned. "Oh . . . his men come to collect the cattle."

"And you've never seen them." I shuffled slightly as her rhythm increased. "The Major handles everything."

She groaned again. "Could this wait? There are more important things . . . oh, God!"

She groaned again, louder and longer, pushing harder, then dropped her head against mine, her lips sucking on my neck as her body shook and slumped against me, a slow satisfied moan coming from her lips.

"Jeez, I needed that." She gasped and resumed a gentle sucking on my neck.

I had to agree that it was nicely timed, though I had been wary of interruptions throughout. My fears were unfounded, while it seemed Rebecca was more intent in continuing her pursuits than talking about the Major or any of the problems I was envisaging. "You really should be going," I insisted, though making no attempt to unlatch her from my neck or disconnect from her warmth. "We don't need you to be discovered here."

She looked up with a devilish smile on her face, kissing my cheek. "You worry too much. I told you, they're all asleep."

"You're not intending to spend the night here?"

"You don't want me to?"

She had to be crazy, or perhaps we both were. "I'd be delighted, only for—"

"I know. Just once more and I'll go . . . promise."

She grinned and set the wheels in motion for another heated session of licentious sex, after which we both lay for some time locked together, silently recovering. It was hard to refuse a woman like Rebecca, but before she became romantically inclined again, I insisted she go, not that I wanted her to, but for her sake. I told her there would be other times, but while the Major was here, it was too risky. She agreed, but only half-heartedly, and I knew she had no intentions of staying away for too long.

Remarkably, after she went, I rolled over and fell into a deep sleep, possibly the best I'd had for some time.

Red woke me the following morning with a growl. I opened my eyes to see him standing at the entrance of the barn looking out, watching as the Major sauntered around his car. I hoped at first he might be going, but after checking the boot and taking something out, he went back inside.

I dressed. My thoughts more on how I would fill in the day now that Rebecca would not be visiting and the Major would surely be keeping a watchful eye on me. I thought it would be better to be away from the homestead, so decided to fit the slasher to the tractor and clear some of the virgin scrub near the field I had ploughed two days before. I wasn't sure it was something that Rebecca would want, but any improvement around the place would surely help.

The changing of the plough and connecting of the slasher took longer than I'd anticipated, as well as a certain amount of cursing, but it was finally achieved, and with Red aboard, I drove the tractor out and towards the field, well away from the house. There was so much could be done with the property, if only Geoffrey had worked at it, but the interest had to be there, and apparently with him, it wasn't.

I reached the area of scrub and started steadily cutting back the foliage and clearing around trees which were too large to succumb to the push of the tractor and the cutting blades of the slasher.

By midmorning, I'd cleared a large area and stopped the machine to rest under the shade of a large gum tree. Red, who had followed me for what seemed miles, was more than happy to join me. As we lazed in the shade, the sound of engines drifted through the air, becoming louder the closer they got.

I stood up and looked in the direction of the noise, walking through the scrub until a large cattle truck towing a horse trailer, followed by an equally large covered truck came into view, making their way through the rugged undergrowth. I watched from behind a tree as the vehicles drove past, Red giving a low growl at the intruders. I counted six men, three in the first truck and three in the second, and wondered how many it would take to round up the cattle and more interestingly, how many it would take to harvest the crop.

I waited until they were gone before moving across to look at the trail they left and thinking to myself they would not be hard to follow and see where they eventually made camp, before returning to the tractor and making my way back to the barn. As I neared the home, I noticed the Mercedes was gone and hoped that the Major had left, though I had doubts. I parked the tractor inside the barn and hopped off, now more interested in following the trucks and seeing what the men were up to. I went to the bike and was about to hop on when Rebecca came into the barn.

"Where have you been?" she asked in an annoyed tone.

"I've been clearing more ground." I paused. "I see the Major's gone?"

"Only into town. He's been acting suspiciously. I saw him come over here earlier. I thought you were here."

"What did he want?" I asked, looking about.

"I'm not sure. He was here for a while before he came back

to the house and said he was going into town."

"How long ago was that?" I asked, a feeling of apprehension coming over me. He was a man who was used to doing what he liked and had already told me to *watch my back,* though I doubted he himself would try anything against me. Then again, I hadn't been here. I looked over at the divan which I had made before leaving. It looked untouched, but now with what Rebecca had said, suspicion was cast over everything. "Did he say where he was going?"

"No. Just that he was going. I didn't ask any questions," she replied. "What are you thinking?"

"He wants me out of here and will do it by whatever means it takes." I moved over to the bed and pulled off the blanket and searched amongst the cushions that made up the divan, finding nothing.

Watching what I was doing, she asked, "What are you looking for?"

"Anything that shouldn't be here. I wouldn't put it past him to plant something here and go to the police.

"Why would he? He'd be running an awful risk with the crop of marijuana nearby."

"Not really. He knows I won't say anything about that for fear you'll get into trouble. So that just leaves . . ." I looked back at the bike. "There's not much here I own."

I moved back to the bike and undid the straps on the saddlebags and opened them. I had few personal items and it didn't take long to pull them out and check, but at the bottom of one bag was a plastic packet containing what looked like dried weed. I pulled it out, holding the bag up and looking at the contents, declared, "That's not mine."

"What is it?" Rebecca asked coming closer to look.

"What do you think?" I handed her the pack and started to put my gear back in the bags, just as the police car pulled up beside the utility. "None too soon," I grumbled doing up the straps and stepping away from the bike. "Let's hope there's no more."

Sergeant Daley got out of the vehicle and looked about, then started to walk towards the barn. "Get rid of that!" I ordered quietly to Rebecca as I started to walk towards the entrance to meet him. "Two visits in a couple of days," I queried, stopping and waiting for him to reach me. "Things must be quiet in town."

"I keep a tight rein on things to ensure the place is quiet," he retorted.

This was his way of telling me this was not a social call.

"Hello, Tom," Rebecca said coming from the shadows and standing beside me.

"Rebecca." He doffed his hat politely.

"What brings you out here again?"

His politeness turned to serious. "There's been talk in town of some stranger selling drugs about the place, so I'm checking all the strangers we know of to find out who."

"And how many strangers are there about at present?" I asked, thinking about how flimsy that excuse sounded.

He ignored the question. "I need to have a look around," he said authoritatively.

"Do you have a warrant?" Rebecca asked, taking us both by surprise and both giving her an astonished look.

"Do I need one?" Tom looked genuinely shocked that she'd even asked.

"No," she replied. "I have no objections. Do you, Richard?"

I shook my head, hoping she wasn't overplaying her part, knowing we'd found only one pack of the weed.

Tom looked about as though unsure where to begin, then went to the bed and did much the same as I had done before deciding there was nothing there. There were so many places things could be hidden in the barn, but that would throw the suspicion more on Rebecca and less on me, so after some milling about, he made a move towards the bike. "Be careful you don't break anything," I warned. "It could be expensive."

He grinned as he looked at the saddlebags. "For you or me?"

I didn't answer, happy to watch as he rifled through, pulling everything out, dumping it on the ground until they were both empty, leaving a bewildered look on his face.

"Happy now?" I asked as he looked about, unsure if he should look further. "You could put it all back."

He ignored my suggestion and turned to me. "Perhaps it wasn't you that they were talking about, but I'll be keeping an eye on you, regardless," he warned.

"Tom, Richard's a hard worker. I think you have the wrong man," Rebecca said.

She stepped between us, prompting Tom to walk out of the barn with her. I watched as she walked to the vehicle with him, then began putting everything back in the saddlebags. The car started up and drove away as Rebecca came back, a smile on her face.

"He was disappointed he didn't find anything on you."

"I'll bet." I looked at her inquisitively. "Where did you hide it?"

She gave a sexy grin. "Like to search me?"

Although the offer was tempting and left me wondering just how innocent this woman was, and I meant that in the kindest way, I reluctantly refused, which brought a disappointed look to her face.

"Go on . . . pretend you're Tom and a big burly policeman. I dare you?" she goaded.

That did it . . .

Chapter Eleven

The body search took hardly any time, Rebecca willingly submitting to strip and reveal where the package was hidden. It was the aftermath which took much longer, and when we were finished, we were both completely exhausted. It was a daring and risqué thing to do in the middle of the day, in an open barn, and although I had my eyes closed at times, my ears were pricked harder than Red's might have been, hoping that the Major didn't arrive back, without us hearing him.

"You should be going," I whispered, not wanting her to, but knowing it was best for all concerned.

"That's all you ever say," she whispered back.

She made no move to dislodge her body from against mine, until I suggested, "You need to go back to the house and act as if nothing has happened. If the Major did send Tom out here, he's not going to be too happy when he finds out he found nothing."

"What are you going to do with that package?" she asked.

"I'll dump it. I'm taking a bike ride shortly, and I'll do it then."

"We could smoke it," she suggested, giving me that wild sexy look she was so good at. "It's been a long time since I visited the land of dreamy high."

"And it will be a little while longer. That would be all we need while the Major's about. Come on." I slapped her playfully on the bottom. "Time to get up."

"Spoilsport," she quipped and lazily slipped off the divan and gathered her clothes, mumbling things about me while she dressed. I hurriedly dressed and walked to the entrance of the barn with her, giving her a quick but passionate kiss before she walked across to the house.

I went back to the divan and remade it so it looked as it was when I'd left that morning, thinking that the Major would make another unheralded inspection of the barn when he returned. Then I hopped on the bike and driving out, down the hill and towards the green gate.

It was easy to see where the trucks had turned off the main track and headed into the bush, so I turned the bike and followed. To the trained eye, it might have been plain to follow the trail, since the drivers were careful not to destroy any of the existing flora, leaving only the wheel tracks which would be overgrown within weeks after they left. How long this had been going on, I don't think even Rebecca knew, but this would be the last time. The tracks led through much of the undergrowth and forested areas of the block, leading to where the split post cattle yard was built.

I stopped the bike in the cover of the timbered area and looked over the scene. There was only the cattle truck with the horse trailer parked near the water. Three horses had been unloaded and were corralled in the yard while four men set up a camp and started a cooking fire not far away. The scene looked completely innocent, and if I hadn't known there was another truck and at least two more men involved, I might have believed they were there only for the cattle.

I pushed off and let the bike coast down to the camp, the men not being alerted until I was nearly there. By the time I'd stopped, two of the men were approaching me, surprised by my arrival. "Can we help you?" the dark-haired chap dressed like a cowboy asked.

"Just checking," I replied, sitting on the bike with one foot on the ground. "I'm working on the property."

"You must be new around here."

"Started a few days ago. You here for the cattle?" I looked over at the truck.

"I would have thought the Major would have told you."

"He mentioned it. I was just checking. Is there anything you want?"

By now, another man had come over while the other stayed back, which was welcome, as he was carrying a rifle, the only gun I'd seen, so far.

"Who are you?" the new arrival asked.

"Richard. And you?"

"They call me Col. That's Ray."

He pointed to the chap I'd been speaking to.

"Smithy, and the fellow with the gun back there is Tex."

"You need a gun to round up cattle?" I asked.

"You never know when you might get a rogue animal. It's for protection."

I looked over at the three horses. "Only three horses to round up all the strays?"

"Ray's the cook. He don't ride anymore," came the answer.

"Have an accident?" I asked Ray.

"Getting too old." He chuckled.

"I thought there would have been more of you. Four doesn't seem enough," I said looking at the group.

"Four's plenty. You staying at the house?" Col asked.

"I bunk in the barn."

"Well away from the owner." Ray grinned. "I've only seen her from a distance. She looks a tasty bit. Have you tried her yet?" He licked his lips.

"No. She's a bit too up herself for my liking," I responded. I didn't want to talk about Rebecca and have him salivating along with his friends.

"We keep our distance," Col broke in. "Probably better if you did much the same with us. We'll be pretty busy from now until we leave."

"And I'm here holding you up." I shrugged. "I'd better let you all get on with it." I started the bike as Col and Smithy turned and walked away.

"I'm here all the time," Ray said quietly. "If you want to come by anytime, we can sit and talk about things." He gave a rude gesture with his tongue and fingers, and grinned.

I reached in my pocket and pulled out the bag of weed that the Major had hidden in my saddlebag, then tossed it to him. "You might have some use for that."

He looked at the bag and his face lit up with a broad smile. "I just might at that."

I gave him a carefree wave and started back the way I'd come, thinking if I didn't know the real reason they were there, they probably wouldn't have been a bad bunch — with the exception of Tex, who looked mean and terribly unsociable.

I double-backed, giving myself a wide berth with the cowboys, hoping the bike motor wouldn't be heard at the camp, and continued on towards the plantation. From there, I made my way through the trees and plants on foot, in the direction of the shed. I moved carefully and quietly, reminiscent of my days in the jungles of Vietnam. I heard men talking before I saw them and approached cautiously. They were standing at the edge of the crop looking at the plants, one complaining it looked like hard work and he was considering going back to the cowboys and getting more help.

"It'll take a week with just the two of us," the smaller of the two grumbled.

"So? You had something better to do?" the other asked. He was taller and looked like he was no stranger to trouble. "Charlie wants us back within the week, crop cleaned out and truck loaded."

"It's all right for Charlie, he doesn't do anything."

"He pays us, so remember that. Now get started while I

back the truck up."

They both walked from the crop, one going to the truck while the other went to the shed and carried out some tools. I made my way back through the crop, satisfied I knew where all the men were now and that the cleanup operation was underway.

I took a long but safe way back to the barn. On arrival I saw the Mercedes was back, parked in its usual place. Rebecca was right about not knowing the men were there. If I hadn't taken the trouble to go and see them, even from the back of the barn overlooking the dam and beyond, I would not have known anyone was on the property.

By now it was getting dark and no one had come from the house. I had heard the children laughing and yelling off and on since I'd arrived, but seen or heard nothing of Rebecca and the Major. I had just lit the lamp when Rebecca came over, a look of worry and concern on her face. "We have to talk," she said, standing in front of me.

I wasn't sure what was coming, but I imagined it was something the Major had instigated. "What seems to be the trouble?"

"Did you tell the Major to leave and not come back?" she asked.

"Is that what he said?"

"Did you?"

"I told him to take the crop and get out, and the next time he came, it would be just to see you and the kids."

Rebecca thought for a moment as though trying to remember the Major's words. "You went too far. You know that. You can't go ordering him off the property. He treats it as his own. He's told me Geoffrey is furious and has also told me to get rid of you." She looked at me as though the words she'd spoken were distasteful.

"Is that what you want?"

"No. You know I don't, but—"

"I was thinking of you and the kids. Once that crop is gone, you have nothing to worry about. What the Major and Charlie do with it once it's off the property is their problem. You have to break the hold he has over you and this place. I don't think Geoffrey knows or cares that much about me, you, or any damn place. I think he's in this drug ring up to his neck, and as long as he's over there and you're here doing as his father tells you, he has nothing to worry about."

"Deep down, I feel you're right, but I don't know. For so long now, he's been helping me—"

"Helping himself and his mates," I contradicted. "How much do you think they make out of a crop that size?"

"How would I know? All I do know is that the money from the agistment goes a long way to keeping us afloat."

"The agistment is only a front. The money comes from selling the crop. Can't you see that? The men arrived today to start rounding up the cattle and clearing the crop. They'll be here for about a week."

"How do you know that?"

"I've been there and spoken to some of them. Granted, they weren't forthcoming with a lot of information, and there was nothing said about the harvesting of the crop."

"Then how do you know they're here to do that?" she asked sceptically.

"Because I've seen the men who are doing it."

"Can you take me there and show me?"

"Definitely not. They're not the sort of men you'd want to hang about with. Actually, a couple of them look downright dangerous." I was thinking of Tex and the bigger of the two men at the crop.

She was weakening, but still uncertain of what she should do.

"How am I going to survive if the cattle go? I don't want to leave here, and it's the only home the children have really known."

"Did you do as I asked and contacted Angus about a crop for planting?"

"Yes, but he hasn't gotten back to me, and whatever we do will take time. I just don't know . . ."

I took her in my arms and held her close. "I'm here to help you, if you'll let me," I whispered gently to her.

She let out a deep sigh. "I want you to, but I'm scared."

"Of what?"

"Everything."

"But not me?"

She looked up, her eyes meeting mine, staring deeply as though reading my thoughts.

"No," she whispered. "Not you. I trust you." Her lips pressed warmly against mine, sending a warm and loving feeling through me.

Our thoughts were ahead of our actions, but sense prevailed, and as much as I would have dearly taken her to the divan, and she would have submitted readily, we both kept our heads. "Are we okay, then?" I asked.

"Better than okay. Do you want to come across for dinner?"

"Will it upset the Major?"

"I should think so," she answered mischievously.

"Good. Let's go," I said taking her hand, pleased that we had overcome another hurdle.

Chapter Twelve

From the look on the Major's face, it was plain to see he hadn't expected to see me again, at least not at the dinner table, and the scowling look that Rebecca received showed that all would not be well in their relationship from here on. It was a silent dinner, broken only a few times by the children asking questions, which Rebecca answered briefly. It was not until the children were told it was time for bed and Rebecca had gone to oversee them that the Major finally spoke to me.

"Is there something going on between my daughter-in-law and you?" he asked. He remained seated at the table, puffing on his cigar.

"The only relationship we have is a working one. She's the boss, I'm just the worker." I knew he was trying to find the reason she hadn't fired me and sent me packing.

He appeared unsatisfied with that answer chomping thoughtfully on the cigar.

"Your friends turned up today, but I suppose you know that?"

"There could still be a job offer there if you're interested."

"We've been there, done that, so, don't go there again."

"Rebecca won't survive here without the handouts I give her."

"Maybe not, but she won't have the problem of being caught up in some police raid and losing everything—children included."

"What makes you so bloody righteous? You've been over in the war zone and seen what goes on. We're just making life a little more comfortable for our boys. There's no harm in doing that."

"Maybe not, if it was legal and you weren't profiteering from it. All the more reason to appreciate what we've got here in this country, provided it's not ruined by characters like you." I felt my voice getting louder.

Rebecca came back into the room, eyeing us both off as she gathered up the dirty dishes. "Keep the noise down, please. If you intend fighting, go outside, I don't want the children kept awake."

I looked over at the Major, and there seemed no reason to continue with the conversation, as neither of us had changed our stance. "I'll retire for the night," I said. I got up, leaving the room. Red dawdled up, following me. I went back to the barn and walked out the back and looked over the dam. There was no sign of fires amongst the trees or any activity, but I knew the men were there and decided to do a reconnaissance the next day to keep an eye on things.

I went back into the barn and settled down on the divan, hoping that Rebecca might pay me a visit. Although I'd told her it was risky and not to, I knew she had a mind of her own.

After an hour of listening to Red whimper and snore as he tossed and turned, I was convinced she wasn't coming and settled down for a restless night. I was beginning to have feelings for Rebecca, not unlike what I had for Eleanor at first. They were two different women, and after Eleanor, I was certainly not in a hurry to become involved seriously with any woman again.

Sleep did not come easily, my thoughts drifting from Rebecca to Vietnam, thinking about what the Major had said about the drugs, and while not denying at times they did help, they could also be a curse and addictive, but our group looked out for each other, so there was little chance any of us would fall wholly under the influence. Beer, of course, was another thing. The large amount that was brought into camp for consumption was nearly as bad, leaving us with a hangover to die for and usually being sick as a dog after a long night on the piss. But that was the nature of the beast. Make hay while the sun shines, because you might not see the next day. Death was always lurking.

I was awake before dawn and went outside to check the sky. A thin wisp of smoke filtered into the sky some distance away so I knew either the cowboys or the crop harvesters were also up and about. It was too early to start the bike and drive over, so I decided on a brisk early morning walk. I was not that keen on Red joining me, but he insisted and tagged along, a few paces behind me. I stayed in the hills on the opposite bank of the creek, knowing I could get a good view of both camps from there.

I reached the first camp as the sun finally lit the sky and started its slow rise above the hills. I could see Ray working over the well-lit fire while the others spent their time saddling the horses and washing in the stream. It seemed that Col was the boss, shouting orders which no one really jumped to. I noticed the covered truck that was at the crop site the afternoon before was stationed not far away, and from beneath that, the two men who were there, got up wearily and went over to the water and washed. They dawdled back to where Ray was serving up some food and took a plate and sat down, soon joined by the rest of the group.

I lay on the grass, partly hidden by bushes, with a commanding view, watching their movements, but unable to hear what was said. Red sat patiently beside me, occasionally giving a low growl, but unsure just what we were doing. Finally they finished eating, and the two got up and went to the truck and drove off in the direction of the crop while the others made their way to the horses and mounted up. Col gave orders to the two men on horseback and yelled something to Ray before the three horsemen rode off into the bush.

I waited a few minutes watching Ray as he cleaned up, taking the plates to the creek and washing them before going back and sitting down at the fireplace. "What do you think, Red? Should we pay him a visit?" Red looked at me haphazardly, but I guessed he really wasn't all that interested. I thought back, remembering there was a place where the stream was shallow and not all that difficult to cross. I wanted my entry to look like I was casually dropping in, not swimming over and clearly showing my intentions.

By the time I reached the crossing, I think Red was bored with all the walking and had probably wished he'd stayed at home or I had brought the bike, but the noise would have alerted everyone to our presence. We made our way along the creek keeping to the bank until I reached the camp. Ray saw me coming, as I was making no attempt to hide, and called out.

"What are you doing here, young fellow?"

He stood up and watched as I approached the camp fire.

"Just out for a morning walk," I answered, hearing Red give a low growl beside me.

"Dog don't bite, does it?" he asked, warily watching Red, before taking a deep draw on the joint he was smoking.

"Not unless he's intimidated," I responded casually looking about. "Where are the rest of the boys?"

"Col and the boys are doing the roundup," he replied. He sat back down again, beckoning me to do the same.

"They gone for long?"

"Probably to midafternoon, depending where the cattle are and how long it takes to get them back here."

"And they leave you here alone. Must be boring for you?"

"Doesn't take much to amuse me at my age." He grinned and handed me an open magazine he'd been reading.

The centerfold left nothing to the imagination. "Wow! Where did you get this?"

He chuckled. "They're American magazines. The boys get them from the yanks in Vietnam. They keep me amused for hours."

"I can see why," I agreed, looking at the centrefold and admiring the raunchy photo. "Col and Smithy are a bit old to be fighting up there."

"No, not them. The boss goes over regularly and brings them back," Ray answered. "Can't get nothing like this over here."

"The boss? That would be Charlie?" I asked, surprised Ray was willing to speak so openly to me—a stranger.

"Do you know him?"

I shook my head. "Only heard about him from what the Major tells me."

"Yea, they're as thick as thieves. Them . . . and that son of his."

Now it was starting to get interesting. I settled down to listen.

"You know Geoffrey?"

"Know of him, but don't like him. Say, where did you get that weed you gave me yesterday?" he asked, feeling in his pocket for the bag I'd given to him. "It's good stuff."

"I came by it." I hedged. "Do you want some more?"

He produced the bag I'd tossed him and looked at the dwindling contents. He thought for a moment. "Should last another day or two, I guess, but I have no shortage of the stuff."

"Is that right? Lucky you."

He smiled, inhaling and exhaling the smoke. "I hope you didn't pay too dearly for this?"

"No. It was given to me, but I have other needs." I grinned.

His eyebrows lifted slightly and he looked at me

inquiringly. "Like what?"

I grinned again and passed him back the magazine, hinting at the naked woman. "I've been away for some time. I've got a lot to make up for."

"Prison?" he queried.

I stayed silent as though unsure whether to say or not.

"Doesn't matter. You're out now. So, are you having it off with the woman at the house?" He gave me a coy smile. "I know *I* wouldn't be holding back."

I smirked. "Hell no. She's my boss. A good looker, though. I wouldn't mind getting into her pants, but—"

He licked his lips. "My sentiments exactly. She's not bad . . . from what I've seen. I wouldn't—"

"I didn't think you chaps ever went up to the house?"

"We're not supposed to, but as you said, it gets boring here at times and I've got a pair of high-powered binoculars in the truck that can see for miles. I've never caught her naked, but . . . you can't stop a chap from imagining what she might be like."

He was nearly slobbering, thinking about Rebecca. I cringed. "I suppose she might affect you like that," I agreed, fully aware of what he was trying to imagine. "I'm curious . . ."

He started to laugh. "Better take another look at that picture, if it's been that long. I'm always curious." He chuckled again.

"Not about that," I said, rejecting the magazine. "Did you see another truck around here yesterday?"

The question caught him by surprise and he stopped smiling and became serious. "What are you talking about?"

"When I was driving back yesterday after meeting you all, I noticed another set of wheel marks on the track. It seemed a bit strange, with only the one vehicle here."

He looked about, then huddled closer as if someone might

hear. "We have another truck come with us to help with the plants."

I looked at him mystified. "Plants? What are you talking about?"

"Charlie and the Major grow marijuana on the property and send it overseas after it's cured, processed and packed," he answered quietly.

"On this property?" I said aloud, as though astounded by that revelation.

"Josh and Ash are over there now clearing the plants. I could get you a job if you want?" He grinned. "I could get you enough weed to keep you high as a kite for a lifetime."

"You old bastard. And I gave you some of mine." I grinned at him.

"And I appreciate that. I'll return the compliment before we leave," he promised.

"When will that be?"

Ray shrugged. "Depends on the cattle and the plants, but as soon as they're all collected, we'll be gone. We don't wait around."

"And what happens after that?" I asked, since we were talking so freely.

"The cattle go to market and the plants are taken back to Charlie's, where they're made ready for Vietnam. Then they bring in more cattle and set up for another crop while they're here. It works like a charm."

"Seems like a lot of messing about, except for the cattle. Why not do all that here?"

He shook his head. "Too many cops. Charlie's place is out in the sticks. Nobody goes near the place. When it's all ready, he flies it to the nearest army base and it's put aboard a transport bound for the war zone. They've got everything sorted out. It's all about who you know." He sniggered at how easy it was.

"That's all right if you can trust everyone, but what happens when it gets there?"

"Strewth, you ask a lot of questions. You could ask the Major, I'm sure he'd tell you," he grumbled as though he'd said enough.

"He's too busy, and I prefer talking with someone like you. The conversation's more down to earth and honest . . . between mates." I slapped his shoulder.

"Yea, I know what you mean. I don't go much for those brass-monkey types myself." He chuckled.

"So, what happens when it gets there?"

"This is just hearsay of course, but the Major's son, Geoffrey, you know him. He has all the contacts over there. Works in some fancy office and liaises with the yanks, so what they don't get rid of to our boys gets sent on to them or the black market. Charlie reckons they can never get enough of the stuff, regardless. They make good money. You should get in with the Major," he suggested, throwing the stub of the joint in the fire.

"No thanks. For someone that doesn't know a lot, you certainly know a lot," I told him, feeling I'd heard the whole story now.

"I sit and listen. They never tell me anything, but I listen. Would you like a drink?"

I looked at my watch and jumped up. "Jeez, look at the time! I'd better get going, Ray, or I'm likely to get the arse. I didn't realise it was this late."

"That's the trouble with having a woman boss — watching the clock and giving orders. I'd like a bit of her arse, though." He smirked with what he was thinking as I started to jog off. "Come back and see me anytime," he called out.

I waved and kept running, Red bounding along at my heels.

CHAPTER THIRTEEN

I was a lather of sweat by the time I reached the barn, thanks to the cloudless sky, humidity and lack of breeze. Red stayed with me until the dam but decided it was cooler in the water and went for a paddle. I can't say I was surprised, though, when I entered the barn to find the Major was there waiting for me. He was standing beside the tractor watching me as I stopped and took a few deep breaths and started to remove the sweat covered shirt I was wearing.

"I would have thought your army training would have held up better than that. You're sweating like a pig," he said distastefully.

"And good morning to you," I answered, disinterested in his remark. "Having trouble finding somewhere to stash more of your little surprises?" I asked, thinking he'd get around to telling me what he was doing there eventually.

"No. No more games. I just came over to say goodbye." He smirked.

"You're leaving?"

"Yes. For a few days. But you won't be here when I get back. It's a shame. You might have been an asset to us if you'd co-operated, but that's the way things go." He shrugged, not elaborating on my premature departure.

"Have you mentioned this to Rebecca?" I asked, wondering what had been said to her about my leaving.

"No. No need. You're like the wind, Scott. People like you blow in and you blow out without at a moment's notice. No one will miss you," he said confidently.

He gave me a cold-blooded look that assured me this time he was not joking.

"Least of all me," he finished.

I looked about, my suspicious mind wondering what he might have booby-trapped or tinkered with, though from experience, I knew it was rare for someone of his rank to do any of their own dirty work. "That's where you're wrong, but thanks for the warning." I tried not to show the concern that was building inside me, so I walked over to the bike and undid the saddlebag and took out another shirt and put it on, looking back at him. "Is there something else you want?"

He gave a snigger and started to walk from the barn. "Good riddance."

I watched as he went out to the Mercedes and got in, taking another look in my direction before starting the car and driving out. I looked at my watch and guessed Rebecca would be in the house, as the truck was in the yard. By now, I should have been out working, ploughing or clearing, but my time spent with Ray and the Major had taken up most of the morning. I went across to the house and knocked on the door.

She must have been standing behind it, as it opened before I'd rapped once. "Has he gone?" she asked looking for the Mercedes.

"Just left. What did he have to say to you?" I asked, moving back, leaning against the verandah rail.

She followed me out and stood in front of me on the verandah. "The usual. He told me you couldn't be trusted. You were just as likely to up and leave without telling me. You were a bad influence and, in the future, if I need help, to ask him." She shook her head. "I don't believe any of what he said, but I am worried for you. I heard him talking to Charlie on the phone and he was arranging something, but he was speaking so low I couldn't hear."

"Charlie does seem to be the brains, but I found out more

about their operation, and your husband is involved up to his ears." There was no soft way of breaking it to her on what I learned from Ray. She should know the truth.

"Who told you that?"

"One of the men Charlie sent down. He seems to know all there is to know. We had a nice little chat. That's why I'm running so late for work this morning." I made it sound like an apology, but in reality, it was something we both needed to know.

"You don't really have to keep to a strict timetable. I'm not a slave driver," she said reaching out and putting her arms about my neck and drawing closer to me.

"That's not really a good idea either," I told her while looking about.

"Why not? We're alone."

"You might think we are, but I happen to know that at times you've had binoculars trained on you, so don't get too amorous when we're out in the open."

"Who?" she asked, looking over my shoulder and seeing no one.

"Let's just say some randy cowboys. If we meet from now on, it should be behind closed doors," I suggested, seeing the worried look on her face.

Her arms slid from around my neck and she stepped back, unsure, but getting the message. "In that case, have you had breakfast?"

"It's a little late for that."

"How about an early lunch? I could use the company."

"I really should be doing something. Did you phone Angus about what to plant?"

She grinned. "Plant? Oh, that! Yes. Come in and I'll tell you what he suggested over a cup of tea."

She took my hand and led me into the house and through to the dining room.

"Take a seat. I won't be a minute."

She went through to the kitchen and returned shortly after with the teapot and two cups. She sat down beside me, placing the cups on the table with the tea and placing her arm around my neck once again.

"Is this private enough for you?"

Her lips searched out mine, kissing me warmly.

"Children?" I asked warily.

"Playing with friends. I took them after breakfast. I'll get them later," she replied.

I should have known once I stepped inside what would happen, noticing the mood Rebecca was in. It was private enough, but not the most comfortable, and as she kissed and fumbled with the buttons of my shirt, I reached behind her and slid down the zipper on her dress.

"Not here," I mumbled, pulling away from her and looking about the room. The table was the most obvious place, but looked and was hard.

"The bed," she whispered, then kissed my cheek, holding me tightly.

I stood and lifted her up in my arms, her dress slowly falling from her shoulders. Bewildered, I asked, never having been any further than the dining room and kitchen, "Where?"

"This way."

She pointed me in that direction as I carried her through along a hallway, past a number of doors and into a room at the end. The large bed dominated the room, while the curtains from the open doors onto the verandah moved slightly in the cool breeze. I walked along the side of the bed and gently deposited her on the thickly padded quilt. As I discarded my shirt and pants Rebecca slipped from the dress and moved over as I lay down, our arms and bodies coming together as though drawn by magnets to each other.

The comfort of the bed only made way for more

uninhibited sex between us, with no restrictions as there was on the divan, and at times, I slowed or stopped my movements as Rebecca's moans became wails. Although we were the only people about, I worried that the sound might carry. But she was in her element, rebuking any attempt to stop or discourage her from achieving her ends. I so admired this determined woman.

It was sometime later as we rested, the sweat glistening on our skin as the cooling breeze that blew in through the open doors did its best to cool our heated bodies that she asked about her husband.

"What part does Geoffrey play in this organisation?"

It was not the ideal topic of conversation I would have preferred after making love to his wife in their marital bed, but it was Rebecca who asked. "I was told he arranges the sale of the drugs and the distribution once it gets to Vietnam."

"Would they be making a lot of money?"

"I would imagine so." I looked up at the ceiling trying to remember how much we paid for a joint or two and the amount the Yanks used to carry with them.

"You'd think he'd send more than a pittance home for me and the children, if that's the case," she said bitterly.

It was not an argument I wanted to become involved with, so I stayed quiet. I'd heard how well some of the ranking officers lived in Saigon and even in Vung Tau with their entertaining, housekeepers and escorts. Life was rough for the elite.

My silence must have mystified her as she rolled on her side, putting her arm across my chest, and smiled at me.

"What are you thinking?"

I smiled back, reaching across and pulling her to me. "How much I like you. How big an idiot your husband is, and finally, how I think I'm falling for you," I whispered, my lips searching for hers, then kissing her passionately.

She broke away, her face bearing a cheeky grin. "You know I'm a married woman . . . with children."

"Who cares?" I grabbed her and rolled over her, hearing her give a girlish giggle before we connected again, silencing any further conversation.

It would be fair to say we were evenly matched, though over time, I'm sure she would have worn me to a pulp if I had not conceded defeat while I could still think straight. She had an insatiable appetite, and I wondered if it was because she had been starved of love over the past two years, or she was out to impress. Regardless, I wanted nothing more than to please her but didn't want to end up dead from the want of trying. It was only when she realised that time had got away on us both that she called a halt to our afternoon of debauchery and suggested a shower to help clean away any of the residues that might cause suspicion. Even then, she was inclined to play more than wash, but I reminded her that her children had yet to be collected, and the afternoon was concluded after drying off and dressing. It was a happy and smiling Rebecca who hopped in the utility and drove off to pick up the children.

I walked back to the barn, wondering where the day had gone, but knowing in some ways it had not been wasted, as it was the happiest I'd seen Rebecca since I arrived. For myself, the more I saw of her, the more I became affected by her charm, looks and . . . everything about her.

I had forgotten everything else. She was the only thing on my mind as I neared the barn and heard the crack, then the wavering sound of the bullet as it whistled through the air not far above my head, slamming into the timber wall of the barn. I instantly dropped to the ground, unsure if it was meant for me or had gone astray while the cowboys were rounding up the cattle. There was no one in sight as I lifted my head and looked about. If it was a warning, it was one I'd be taking heed of. I waited. Listening, but hearing nothing more. I slowly stood and scampered into the barn, stopping as I entered, taking cover behind the wall before looking out.

I had nothing but a knife and wasn't sure if Rebecca had a gun of any type in the house, but thought she should, being in the country and with a husband in the services. Nothing more happened, and I saw nothing in the vicinity from where the shot came. I'd seen Tex with a rifle, but being cowboys, there was probably more than one.

Was this what the Major had warned me about? Was it a warning, or an accident? How desperate were these men and what would be the consequences if I remained here at the farm? Were they capable of killing in cold blood? These thoughts and more raced through my mind as I moved about in the barn, feeling safe, but ever wary. If I was to leave, what would happen with Rebecca and the kids? Could I trust the randy Ray—or any of those men, for that matter—to stay away? If the Major was here, that would ensure her safety, but he was gone for a few days, or so he said. And was that shot something to do with the arrangement he had made with Charlie on the phone, which Rebecca had overheard? Life was suddenly becoming complicated again.

I found a quiet dark corner near the hay bales and sat down. I needed to talk with Rebecca, though I worried anything I said about that shot might panic her, and I didn't want that. Besides, there were the children to think about as well, but it was me they were after—if that shot was meant for me? I couldn't just up and leave her. That wasn't me. After my last fight, I wanted nothing more than a tranquil lifestyle and not to be hunted by some local drug cartel. I shook my head and wondered how the hell I got myself into these situations.

My arm and shoulder ached, followed by my leg, reminding me of the last fight—one that we didn't win either. A search and destroy mission, but the command had thought there was little chance of finding anything, which set our minds at ease. Patrols were always a tense and anxious time. Booby traps, snipers, ambush. Anything was always a possibility, so we were always alert—always keeping a watchful eye out for anything that moved, looked disturbed or out of the ordinary. But there was always that chance . . .

I heard Rebecca return in the utility, the kids get out, laughing and talking as they always did until they went inside the house, and the silence prevailed again.

Chapter Fourteen

I was still sitting on the bales of hay when Toby came across to tell me dinner was ready. At first he didn't see me sitting in the shadows, until I coughed.

"Why are you there?" he asked, coming over to me. "If you're tired, you should be on your bed."

I smiled. "Sometimes it nice to just sit in the dark and listen to the quiet."

He looked confused. "I don't hear anything?" He paused to listen, then remembered why he came. "Mum said dinner's ready."

"Best we go," I said. I stood up, brushing off any loose straw, before tidying myself up as we walked out of the barn. Shadows of night were starting to fall as we entered the house and I took my place at the dinner table. Red welcomed me back after being absent for the day and leaving me that morning. Rebecca still retained her happy mood from the afternoon and it appeared to be shared by the children as they talked and laughed. It was different when the Major was there, him dominating the conversation with the children speaking only when spoken to.

"Did you do much work today?" Helen asked while she waited for her mother to bring the dinner.

"Not as much as I would have liked," I lied.

"What were you doing?" Toby enquired.

That was the one question I didn't want. "A bit of this and that," I said fobbing off the question as best I could.

"He was listening to the quiet when I went and got him,"

Toby told his sister.

"What?" She made a face, indicating she didn't understand.

"I was resting," I explained.

"But not on the bed," Toby informed her.

"Why not?" Helen asked, still confused.

"Why not, what?" Rebecca asked.

She had just come from the kitchen, carrying the dishes and coming to my rescue once again.

"Richard was telling us what he did this afternoon," Toby spouted out.

I saw Rebecca's face whiten and, for a moment, I thought she was going to drop what she was holding. Instead, she looked at me for direction, then smiled, putting the dishes down on the table.

"He worked very hard. I'll bet he didn't tell you that?" She winked at me, satisfied she'd resolved the issue.

"Is that why you were resting?" Helen asked, as though everything we'd spoken of had fallen into place.

"Pretty much," I agreed, pleased when Rebecca finally sat down beside me and we started to eat, turning the conversation from me to food.

It was one of the most enjoyable dinners we'd had together. The children were talking and laughing about what they'd done at their friends' place, with Rebecca and me joining in, asking questions, which they answered truthfully and, in some cases, hilariously. It reminded me of my childhood, or at least pieces of it. Afterward, they obediently went to bed as they always did, though this night they both said goodnight to me before they went. I sat at the table, waiting for Rebecca to return, sipping the tea and thinking how much I'd enjoyed the dinner with her family. I couldn't recall the last time I'd actually sat down with my family and enjoyed dinner as much. Probably never . . .

"The children are getting to know you," Rebecca said when she came back, sitting down beside me. "Helen likes you." She grinned and gave me a wink. "Toby's still undecided, but coming around."

"They are good kids," I commented, putting down my cup and turning to her. "You don't, by any chance, have a gun here in the house?"

She looked at me strangely. "What brought that on?"

"I merely asked." I struggled to come up with a plausible explanation. "I think there are a few rats in the barn. I hear them at night. I thought you'd have something, being here in the bush."

She seemed relieved with what I said. "There's a rifle hanging over the fireplace in the lounge room, but I'm not sure it works. It's been there for as long as I can remember."

"And that's it?" I gave her an inquiring look.

"Look. If you're interested, you can come and sleep in my bed if you're worried about rats. So long as you've left before the children wake. I certainly don't mind."

Her arm reached out and wrapped about my neck as her lips sought mine. It was a warm and loving kiss, but not one I thought appropriate for here or for now.

I broke away, looking towards the hallway entrance. "The kids?"

"They're probably both asleep. They sleep soundly," she whispered, wanting more.

"And that's the only gun?" I asked, trying to remain on the one topic.

She pulled back and looked at me strangely. "What is this sudden infatuation with guns?"

"I just thought—"

"Geoffrey had some sort of a pistol, but I'm not sure what he did with it." She looked at me suspiciously. "Is there something you're not telling me?"

"No!" I replied, possibly too quickly.

She hesitated, staring at me, saying nothing.

"I just wanted to know, but if it worries you, forget about it. The rats can live on for a few more nights."

"I can get some poison from the store," she offered.

"Not with the dogs about. I'll come up with something."

"In the meantime, the offer of sleeping with me is still open," she whispered, her face and her lips returning, warmly pressing against mine.

This time I let it happen. It seemed like an eternity before we finally broke from the clinch, looking deeply into each other's eyes and wanting this to continue, but knowing there was more to do.

"Will you accept my offer?"

I nodded. "I'd love to, but what if the Major returns?"

"I can't see a problem. If you come around the verandah, my room is the first you'll reach. My doors are usually open, so come in. I'll be waiting. We can practice while he's not here." She grinned deviously.

I had no answer to that, and it seemed Rebecca had given it some thought, though the problem of the guns still worried me.

"Why don't you go back to the barn, give me some time to clean up here and get ready and when you return, we'll have a glorious night of . . ."

She didn't have to spell it out. Her lips closed warmly over mine again, not that I was about to argue with her idea. On the contrary, I was more than receptive.

Red came with me back to the barn. I hadn't lit the lantern before I left and I had no intentions of doing it now. I had other thoughts on my mind. I took off my shirt and found a black skivvy in the saddle bag and slipped it on, followed by the black balaclava I sometimes wore under the bike helmet for warmth. It had been a humid day and the night so far had been no exception, but I felt the dark clothes would be more appropriate for what I had in mind. I strapped the knife scabbard to my belt and took out the knife, checking the blade before returning it to the leather sheath. I was hoping I'd have no use for it, but it was better than nothing and let me feel that I at least had some weapon for protection.

"You can come, Red, but you'll have to be quiet," I told the dog who was watching me closely. "There'll be no time for a swim."

He whimpered as though he understood and followed me as I walked out of the barn and headed down the hill towards the dam. There was no moonlight — only what the night sky allowed, but that was how I wanted it. In the distance, there was the odd flash of lightning and I reasoned we could get a storm before morning. I crossed the creek at its shallowest place and made my way to the far bank, Red enjoying the water as I knew he would, then continued on, following the creek until I neared the cowboy's camp.

The covered van was parked near the cattle truck, so I knew they were all there. The fifty or so cattle they had penned in the yard stood silent as I made my way past, keeping in the shadows and finding myself a convenient place to hide and watch the camp. Red was quiet as he settled down beside me. Five of the men were sitting around the fire, smoking, and drinking, talking aloud as men do when there's no fear of being overheard. Ray was there, relaxing like the rest and seemingly out of the conversation. I wasn't sure which one was missing, either Josh or Ash, but the bigger of the two men collecting the crop was whinging to the others.

"Another pair of hands would be a help," he complained. "It's going to take longer than you all think. The plants are large and going to seed — tacky as all shit. Ash is pissed off that it's starting to seep through his gloves — it's that bad."

"We got a few more days finding and rounding up the cattle," Col countered, finishing off his beer and reaching for another.

"Bullshit! Look at how many you've got in the yard. I could have brought them in by myself. You just don't want to get your hands dirty," Josh persisted.

"Shut your whining," Tex growled. "You're paid to do what you do, so shut up and do it."

Josh scowled, but said nothing, preferring to puff on the joint until he spat it out and stood up. "Fuck it. I'm going to sleep," then walked off towards the truck.

"Good thing," Col mumbled. "A paddock full of weed and he's still not happy."

"You want I should do something about it?" Tex asked, staring at the fire.

"No. Not yet, anyway. Let them get done on what they have to do. They're both a pair of idiots. I don't know why Charlie sent them. Besides, you have your work to do."

"Is that really necessary?" Smithy asked.

"You mind your business and I'll take care of mine," Tex told him coolly. "If he's still there tomorrow . . . I'll see he's missing in action. A definite shame, but . . ." He shrugged.

"I like the chap," Ray said incoherently, draining the last of his beer and tossing the can away.

"I reckon it's time you hit the hay, Ray. You've had more than enough," Col told him. "You've got an early rise in the morning."

"I have an early rise every damned morning and never have anywhere to put it," he grumbled and laughed at his attempted humour, trying to stand and nearly falling on the fire, saved only by Col's quick hands. "Shit! Thanks. The fire moved."

"Get to bed, old man," Tex ordered in a gruff and commanding voice.

"Bite your . . ." Ray grumbled as he staggered a few feet away and fell down on a blanket already set out on the ground.

"Silly old bugger," Tex growled, standing up as though ready to take action against him. He looked at where Ray had fallen and was now snoring loudly.

"Leave him. I think we'd all better get some sleep. Looks like we could be in for a storm at some time," Col said looking at the distant sky.

"I'll be in the truck. Wake me for breakfast," Tex said picking up his rifle and going over to the cattle truck and opening the door of the cab.

"That guy gives me the creeps," Smithy said quietly to Col.

"He gets paid to cover our arse and eliminate any problems. He's a necessary evil," Col answered, speaking just as quietly. "I'm off as well. I couldn't sit here listening to Ray snore like that."

"What about him?" Smithy asked, looking over at Ray. "The storm?"

"He'll wake up when he gets wet enough. Serves him right for getting so stoned." Col stood and moved off to the truck and Smithy, seeing there was no one left, followed.

Listening to this conversation told me what I suspected about Tex. His attitude, as cold as the words he spoke, left me in no doubt the shot that whistled over my head was a warning, but what was to come might be more permanent.

The area went quiet except for Ray's snoring, and I waited until I felt the rest of the men were asleep before slowly moving from my hiding place. "Wait here," I told Red as I made my way to the covered van, checking out the two men sleeping at the back of the van under a tarp, the smell of the plants being enough to keep them high. I crept over and found Col and Smithy asleep under the truck and knew that Tex was asleep in the cab. What I needed to know was what arsenal of weapons they had and where they might be, and I knew the one person who would know everything.

I heard the first sounds of rumbling as I made my way back to Ray, keeping low and sliding over the ground until my head was nearly touching his. He reeked of booze and whatever else he'd been smoking or drinking and the smell was nearly unbearable. I squeezed his nostrils, preventing him from both snoring and breathing and listened as he gargled and gulped until his eyes opened and he looked directly up at me. I released his nostrils and held his head firmly.

"Who the fuck are you?" he spluttered, unsure what his eyes were seeing.

"I'm your worst nightmare. I'm the grim reaper here to take your soul if you don't tell me what I want to know," I said in a husky deep voice.

His eyes stayed wide open as he swallowed deeply. "Are you kidding me?"

"Do I look like I'm kidding?"

His eyes were glazed and I wasn't sure what he was actually seeing or believing, but I felt him swallow deeply before he nervously asked, "What?"

"Where are the guns?"

"Guns?"

"Where do you keep the guns?"

"In the truck . . . the cattle truck."

"Where?"

"Some in the cab and more in the dog box. Why? Why do you want to know?"

"You do know it's going to rain?"

"When?"

He couldn't look up as I was holding his head.

"Am I likely to get wet?"

"If you close your eyes and go back to sleep, I'll make sure you're protected from any danger."

"Would you? That's nice of you," he murmured, then closed his eyes as I'd asked.

I waited, and before long his snoring again reverberated around the camp. I crept over to the truck and lifted myself onto the running board and looked in. Tex was asleep on the seat, his gun lying alongside him. I thought about reaching through the window and taking the rifle, but he seemed too attached to it and I thought it might be more than enough trouble to relieve him of it. I stepped back on the ground and moved along to the dog box at the side of the truck and carefully opened the door, keeping a close eye on Col and Smithy as I unlatched it.

It was a smorgasbord of firepower, ranging from handguns to the latest army style automatic weapons, more than I could carry and much more than four cowboys would need to round up a couple of hundred head of cattle. Why they would require this amount of artillery baffled me, but at least it would alleviate my problem of defending myself. I carefully extracted two of the rifles and two of the handguns and placed them on the ground. *M16's and hardly used.* The same as the handguns. Someone had a friend in the American camp, obviously. I'd handled them when off duty in Vietnam, but as the SLR — semi-automatic Self-Loading Rifle — was our weapon of preference, I'd had little more to do with them. I searched about for additional ammunition and found what I considered would be plenty, shoving a number of clips in my pockets. Col must have been having a bad dream and tossed himself about recklessly. I froze, but luckily, he didn't wake, just settled again.

I contemplated what to do with the additional guns, not wanting to leave them there, and so decided to gather up what I could and take them downstream and deposit them in the water, well away from the camp. At least it cut down the odds against me if it came to an all-out fight, but there was no way I could find out how much more firepower there was inside the cab of the truck. On my return, I closed the dog-box and collected the guns I'd put aside and made my way back to where Red was waiting. By now, the lightning was getting closer and the thunder rumbled continuously, though as yet there was no rain. I looked around the camp again. Nothing seemed out of place to what it was when I'd arrived, except for Ray who was still sleeping peacefully. It seemed a shame to leave him in the open as he was, but I doubted he'd remember a thing by morning.

I started off, moving silently through the camp and along the bank feeling the first few drops of rain. I was pleased and welcomed the rain to cool off the air and also cover my tracks, although they'd know when they discovered the guns missing who it was likely to be. I hurried on, Red keeping by my side until we reached the shallows of the creek, where he lagged behind, but he caught me again as I was making my way up the hill towards the barn. By now, the rain was falling and the thunder and lightning were performing together, lighting the way and hiding any noise we made.

Inside the barn, I removed the balaclava and looked around for a place to stash the guns and ammunition — not together, but handy. Red shook himself and made his way to his bed and curled up, his way of getting warm and hiding from the storm. After concealing the guns and ammunition, I made my way across to the house and onto the verandah. I was saturated, but a change of clothes wouldn't have helped, since it was now pelting down as heavy as on that first day the storms appeared. I quietly made my way to the French doors that were open and moved the curtains and entered. "Richard?" Rebecca called softly.

"Yes. Sorry," I answered, trying to get out of my wet clothes.

"What kept you? I was beginning to think you weren't coming. I finished cleaning up hours ago."

"I had a few things I had to do," I replied tossing my wet clothes onto the verandah.

"Close the doors. We don't want to be disturbed," she said.

CHAPTER FIFTEEN

The storm raged for hours, the rain hammering down on the iron roof of the house, drowning out any cries emitting from Rebecca's lips. The large bed had definite advantages over the small divan, as we wrestled and cavorted, stirring up a storm of our own in the bedroom. By sunrise it was over, the storm outside blowing out and giving rise to clear skies and what looked like another warm day, while inside, I awoke knowing I'd had little to no sleep, but had to get dressed and leave before the children woke and discovered me in their mother's bed.

I dressed quickly. My clothes were still damp and would have to be changed again when I reached the barn. I let Rebecca sleep, giving her a tender kiss before leaving by the French doors and making my way back to the barn. Red was just waking, giving a yawn that nearly swallowed himself and looking at me as though wondering where the devil I'd been all night. I changed again, hanging out the damp clothes to dry while considering my options for the day. I wasn't sure who would make the next move, but I wanted to make sure I was ready. I went around the barn checking the guns I'd hidden now that it was daylight, and put the Browning pistol in my belt, covering it with my shirt. At least now I wasn't unprepared.

It was the day to work inside the barn, making sure I wasn't a target for Tex working outside. I heard Rebecca start the utility and drive down the hill taking the kids to the bus. I knew that later she'd come to the barn and invite me for breakfast, so I dallied about clearing more room and tidying up until I heard the utility return with a screech of brakes. I walked to the entrance in time to see her come running from the truck, looking back down the hill and throwing herself into my arms. "Are you all right?" I asked, looking back at where she'd come from unsure what had scared her.

"There was a man down by the creek. He had a gun and pointed it at me," she said hurriedly.

"He fired a shot at you?"

"No, but I thought he was going to. He just stood there and raised the gun at me."

"What did he look like?" I asked looking outside but seeing no one.

"Tall, straggly blond hair to his shoulders, with the weirdest, eyes . . . creepy. On his head, he wore a large cowboy hat." She shuddered.

"That's Tex," I answered. "He didn't follow you?"

"I don't think so. I panicked and put my foot to the floor." She seemed surprised. "Do you know him?"

"I met him the other day when I went to their camp. He didn't impress me either, but I am surprised he did that to you."

"He scared the hell out of me. Why would he do that?"

"As you said, trying to scare you. It's me he's after, so let's get you back to the house where you'll be safe," I said, taking her hand and running with her out of the barn and across the grass to the house, Red joining in, unsure what was happening but not wanting to be left out. She opened the door off the verandah and we both went in, waiting as Red took his time to enter.

"Why will I be safe here? And what about you?" she asked as the door closed.

"They wouldn't dare harm you. They'd have to answer to the Major and Charlie. As for me . . . I'm expendable. The

Major doesn't want me about. I'm making waves, so he intends to sink me."

"What do you mean, *sink*?"

"From what I heard last night, I gather Tex has been told to get rid of me—one way or the other."

"Kill you?" Her face was a mask of horror.

"If I don't leave and let them continue as they are."

"But . . . but . . . they can't do that."

"We're dealing with drug dealers, Rebecca. They're a law unto themselves. We either let them continue what they're doing, or we call a halt to it now."

"You said you heard something last night. Where were you?"

Her tone told me the conversation was becoming too much for her to comprehend. "I went to their camp and spied on them for a while."

"That's why you were so wet—and late?"

"I needed to know a few things," I said, neglecting to mention the guns.

She appeared shocked, although it should have dawned on her that anyone who defied the Major could find themselves in a spot of trouble.

"Oh, shit . . ."

She took my hand and walked me to her bedroom. It was not really the time to re-enact the night before, although it certainly would have taken my mind off what I was thinking.

"Over in the drawer," she continued, prompting me to go to the bedside table. "I found it this morning, but I don't know a lot about it."

I opened the drawer and looked down at the long cylindrical object and turned to her, unsure. I took it and held it up. "What do you want me to do with it?" I grinned.

"Not that."

She hurried over to me and took the vibrator from me, a

sheepish grin on her face.

"The gun."

I took another look and saw the metal partly covered by a pair of silk panties. It was a service revolver, possibly from the Second World War, but loaded, and looked like it had been kept in reasonable condition. "This is your husband's?"

"I'm not sure. His, or the Major's. Does it work?"

"Without firing it, I'd say it has a fifty-fifty chance."

"You can take it, if it will help."

She looked at me, then the gun.

"I'm sorry I got you involved in this. If I'd have known, I never would . . ."

I put my finger to her lips and shushed her quietly. "You haven't forced me into anything. You needed help, and I offered. We'll see this through, together."

"What are we going to do? Should we phone the police?"

It was something I had considered, with Rebecca's safety always on my mind, but with my knowledge of Sergeant Daley, he'd probably arrest me and forget about the bad guys. I knew from the conversation around the fire the night before that Tex and Col would probably be my main adversaries, since the rest didn't seem willing to cooperate in any violence. "I think I can handle it," I told her. "But I want you to stay here in the house. Don't go outside."

"But I'll have the children to collect this afternoon."

"I'll try and bring it to a close before then."

"How?"

"Just do as I ask . . . please." I gave her a kiss, nothing to get her excited about, but enough to show her I cared deeply for her. "I've got to go. Stay inside." I opened the door and looked out, but could see no one. I hurried out, closing the door and raced across to the barn. What was I going to do? I had no idea, but my one thought was if I could eliminate my opposition numbers, I would stand a better chance. I knew where Ray and the two plant collectors were, so I'd start with them. I still carried the pistol and went and retrieved one of the M-16's I'd hidden and gave it a quick check before securing it on the bike. I knew where Tex was, or the vicinity he was in, so chose to go the opposite way and cross the creek at the shallows.

I kicked the bike into action and sped out the doors leading to the dam, then followed the creek, crossing in the shallows and making my way to the camp. Ray was there puttering about and stopped as I came into view. I drove steadily towards him, but he waved his arms and came running towards me. "What are you doing here?" he asked looking about. "It's not safe for you to be here."

"Why's that?" I asked, having a fair idea.

"Tex is out to get you. You really should just get on your bike and ride. He's one mean son-of-a-bitch when he gets riled, and at present, he's not happy. I wouldn't like you to tangle with him," he said.

"Where are Col and the boys?" I asked brushing his concerns aside.

"In the hills somewhere. Why?"

"It would be best if you all packed up and left. The cops will be swarming all over this place in the next couple of hours."

"Cops? How come? Charlie always said the place was safe and protected?" He stood, scratching his head, unsure

I hadn't been sure about Daley being in the Major's pocket, but that statement sort of convinced me. "I don't know about that, but that's the word I have."

"Shit! I don't know how to contact them, and there's the cattle." He looked over at the yard with the cattle that had been rounded up.

"Let them go. Your main job here is the marijuana, isn't it?"

"Yea. I guess. I'll have to warn Josh and Ash."

"I can do that, if you release the cattle and get that truck out of here. I wouldn't want you to get caught up in a drug bust," I told him, making my voice sound as authentic as anyone hoping to lessen the numbers on some opposing team.

"You're all right, fella. I'll do that, while you warn the others," he said, nodding his head and agreeing to what sounded like a good plan.

I watched as he went over to the yard, then I drove off following the creek, stopping the bike near the van. There was little noise as I walked around the back of the shed, where I was confronted by Josh, the larger of the two men.

"Who the hell are you?" he asked, not having been introduced to me before.

"Richard. I work on the property. I've been talking with Ray. There's going to be a raid on the property within an hour. He told me to tell you two to get to hell out of here. He's leaving with the truck as soon as he releases the cattle."

"What?" He looked at me with disbelief. "But we haven't finished. We're only about half way." He scratched his head and looked back at the cleared area of land within the trees.

"What's going on?" Ash asked, walking from the bush and standing beside Josh.

"There's going to be a police raid on the property," Josh repeated.

"Who says?"

"Ray was telling me. He sent me here to tell you two to pack up and go," I answered. I sensed that Ash would be the one who would want to leave.

"What did Col say?" Ash asked.

"Col wasn't there. Perhaps they've got out of the place on horseback," I suggested.

The two men looked at each other. "Col's the boss. What do you think?" Ash asked.

"Ray's probably stoned again. This morning over

breakfast, he was raving on about some grim reaper that was talking to him last night. He didn't make a lot of sense then and this doesn't now," Josh said, scratching his head and eyeing me off.

"Hey. I'm only the messenger. When I'm done here, I'm off. I'm not going to get caught here. Do you know how many years you can get for growing and selling this stuff? And you guys have a truckload of it. Good luck with that if you get caught," I told them turning and walking back to the bike.

"We don't know you from a bar of soap. Why should we believe you?" Josh yelled out.

"You don't have to. Keep doing what you're doing until the cops arrive—that should convince you. Or you could go back and check with Ray if he's still there." I hopped back on the bike and kicked the engine into life, watching as they talked about their situation between themselves. I gave them a wave and drove off in the direction of the camp, hoping that by now Ray would have left. The whole thing was a bluff, but if I could reduce the numbers, I might stand a chance against them.

I reached the camp and saw the cattle wandering about with no sign of the truck and knew Ray had done as I asked. I drove on, leaving the creek and going onto the tracks where the vehicles had come in. The tire marks from the truck were easily distinguishable after the rain. It seemed pointless searching for Col and the riders, as they could have been anywhere in the hills. My main concern was Tex. He had scared Rebecca and taken a warning shot at me. He was the danger, though there was Col, but the others didn't seem to have the heart for a fight.

I was nearing the end of the forested section and before long would reach the creek where Tex had been standing when Rebecca was returning. I slowed the bike, then stopped, the foliage affording me plenty of cover as I looked along the track. The truck was nowhere in sight, but there was an uneasy calm about the place. A chill went through me, remembering that last engagement in Vietnam. Not a sound. Not a bird singing or fluttering of their wings. Just calm.

Taking the handlebars, I pushed the bike off the track and into the thickly overgrown area and removed the rifle, setting off on foot. I asked myself question after question. What was I doing? Was this a continuation of the war, but only on home soil? Was I plain bloody stupid? The last time I did this there were nineteen of us, this time one — me! If it was only Tex I was stalking, the odds were good, but if there were more . . .

A branch fell from a tree, knocking against other branches as it fell until it thumped onto the ground. Instinctively, I dived for the ground, looking up to see where it had fallen from, my finger on the trigger. Silence! If Tex was close by, he was being as careful and cautious as me. My eyes scanned the tree line for movement. Nothing. I carefully rose from the dirt and foliage, watching for any movement. It was all coming back to me, that time over there. Each step I took now, I checked, not that I expected a booby-trap, but I wasn't sure how proficient Tex might be. If he was a killer, had he been taught by some of the best in the business?

As the foliage thinned, I caught a glimpse of the truck, stopped just past the creek, and I could see Ray sitting on the footstep of the truck hunched over as though in pain.

CHAPTER SIXTEEN

It seemed strange that Ray was just sitting there, but on closer scrutiny, he appeared to be in agony, hunched over, holding his arm or chest. I couldn't be sure what had happened, but to me, it seemed like an old decoy trick where a person in pain was used to lure the unwary to him and you had your second victim. Something the VC had done quite successfully during my time at the war. There was not enough cover for me to reach him without being seen, and to wait till nightfall would be too long. Besides, Rebecca would have the children to collect that afternoon. I scanned the surrounding area. If Tex was hiding close by, he was well camouflaged.

I waited. At least Ray wasn't calling out for help, but with the heat, and his injuries unknown, I felt it might not be long before he did. What I hadn't expected was the two horsemen who rode out of the scrub and cantered towards the truck.

As they got close, one dismounted and hurried across to Ray and spoke with him, standing up and looking about.

"What fucking stupid game are you playing?" he called out aloud.

For a moment, there was silence and nothing moved, then, from a clump of bushes some distance away, Tex slowly stood up, branches of the bush attached to his upper body and hat. "He's an arsehole," Tex shouted back and strode towards the group of men.

"You cut him up," Col hollered, looking at the wounds.

"He's lucky I didn't shoot him."

It was plain to see they were both hot under the collar and continued shouting at each other. "Your orders were clear. That doesn't mean you practice on the boys."

"He was leaving. What did you expect me to do?" Tex said, defending his actions.

Col, for a moment, looked mystified at Ray, then said to Tex when he reached him, and as he too looked down at Ray. "It wasn't his fault, you maniac. It was the bloody farm hand. You didn't have to do that to him. He needs a doctor,"

"He'll live. Give him a joint. That will help with the pain." He chuckled.

As they were having their lively discussion, Josh and Ash drove along the track and, seeing the truck and everyone, slowed down and stopped. "What's going on?" Josh yelled out.

"What the hell are you two doing here?" Col called out, convinced he was dealing with a pack of idiots.

"We were told to get out of here. The cops are going to raid the place."

"Bullshit! Who told you that? No. Let me guess — that bloody farmhand bastard," Col cursed and looked at Tex. "What are you going to do, shoot them as well?"

"No. I'll get the bastard who instigated all this." Tex spat out.

"See you do. He's a thorn in my side as well as yours." He looked at Josh. "You two get back to work and hurry it up. Smithy, get here and take Ray and the truck back to the camp and see if you can stitch him up while you're there. I'll bring your horse when I come," Col added, throwing orders about.

What I'd hoped for had been dashed. They were all returning to the camp, and this time I'd be a target for any of them. The van turned around and started back down the track while Smithy helped Ray back into the cab, then got in and started the truck. Col pulled Tex to one side and was talking with him, the noise of the truck drowning out anything I might have heard. I watched as the vehicles returned down the track, thinking how close I'd come to splitting the group.

Tex pointed towards the house and I heard Col say something to the effect that he couldn't go there.

"It's off limits," Col said shaking his head. "You're not to touch the woman or the kids. Understood?"

"It would make it so simple," he complained.

"If they find the body, it has to look like an accident," Col warned.

"They won't find a body. I've got a place already picked out for him."

"I don't want to know. Just get the job done. We've found most of the cattle. We should get them in by tomorrow, so you've got two days," Col told him.

"Gimme Smithy's horse and I'll ride back with you. I've blown my cover here now so there's no sense hanging about," Tex grumbled, putting his rifle over his shoulder and walking over to the horse and getting onto the saddle. He waited while Col did the same before they both rode off back down the track following the trucks.

I lay quietly until some time after the noise of the truck and horses had gone. Tex was no amateur, and I realised I was not to underestimate him. Like most things to do with Charlie, I guessed Tex was all army and had taken his training as seriously as I had in my time. It would now be a battle of wits, where one false move could bring either of us undone. I sat up slowly, got to my feet, feeling disappointed. I would now have to come up with another plan if I was going to put an end to this. I went back, uncovered the bike and set off for the barn, unsure of my next move.

Rebecca was there before I hopped off the bike, running up to me and throwing her arms around my neck. "Are you all right?" she asked looking closely at me.

It was probably the dirt on my face and clothes that might have panicked her, but I had no injuries — only fractured pride.

"I'm fine, just a bit frustrated," I said enjoying the warmth of her breath against my face as her hand brushed away grains of dirt.

"I can help you with that." She grinned, then kissed me sweetly.

It seemed Rebecca had the solution to all my troubles and frustrations as my thoughts of Tex and Col disappeared momentarily. The glitch was that it was only temporary as the problems came looming back as she broke away and the warmth of her lips on mine dissipated.

"Come to the house and have some lunch. You can tell me what happened this morning while we eat."

That was a welcome invitation, so I got off the bike, brushed down my clothes, and took her hand. After hearing part of the conversation between Col and Tex about Rebecca and the children, I felt somehow relieved that they were not to be harmed and felt she was relatively safe as long as she remained at or near the house.

While we dined, we talked. I told her what had happened that morning, how I had attempted to split the group but didn't quite succeed and how Ray had been injured, although I wasn't sure the extent of his wounds. What I neglected to tell her was that I was their target, because I didn't want her to panic. It was not the first time I'd mentioned it to her, but before I only supposed it to be true. This time I was sure.

"Why don't you leave? Go. Let them do what they want and come back in a week or a month's time," she suggested.

"That's not going to solve the problem. You need to put a stop to this now. I leave, and the problem will continue. A new crop will be grown and the whole thing will be repeated. The Major will come and go, just to oversee that you're behaving yourself and nothing will change. Is that what you want?"

"No. I want *you*." She went silent for a moment. "Why don't we pack up, collect the children and drive somewhere?"

"Where?" I asked impulsively. "It takes a lot to start your life over from scratch."

I remembered what I'd had before being drafted and what I had now. It was a shock to the system, and although the children might have enjoyed the struggle, I wasn't sure Rebecca would. "You're better off to stay here. You have friends, the school and your home. You just need to get rid of the stench."

"Why not let me phone Tom and explain everything to him? I'm sure he'll listen. Then let him sort out the mess," she suggested.

"He's convinced I'm a bad guy, thanks to the Major, and I'm worried the police might think you're involved with that crop. It is on your land."

"But I didn't know anything about it."

"Would the Major back you on that?" I asked.

"Of course." She thought for a moment. "I suppose he would — wouldn't he?" she asked me doubtfully.

"He'll look after himself, then his son, maybe you or possibly the children in that order. If someone had to be sacrificed, it's more likely to be you," I warned.

"Tom wouldn't believe that. He knows me," she replied nervously.

"I heard from one of the men that the place was protected.

I could only assume he meant by the police."

"Rubbish. Tom's as straight as they come. I can't believe he'd be involved in anything crooked."

I shrugged. "Everyone's entitled to their opinion. You can have yours about him, but I'll reserve mine."

"So, what do we do?"

"You do nothing. Stay around the house as you'd normally do and keep an eye on the children. They don't need to know. I'll try and bring the whole thing to a head. I can't afford to wait for them to make a move," I said, unsure how much time I might have to put any plan into action.

"What are you going to do?"

"I don't know, but it was always said the best plan for defence is attack, so I'm thinking a few surprises could make a difference to our situation."

"What do you mean?"

"If we cause a major disruption to what they're doing, they might just pack up and leave."

"A disruption?"

"They're here for one reason, and it's not the cattle. If that was eliminated, they'd have nothing to stay here for," I said, forming a plan in my mind.

"You're talking about destroying the marijuana crop?"

"Does that worry you?"

"No. But how?"

"I'm not sure. They have half the crop in the van and the rest is yet to be harvested."

"Won't they be guarding everything?"

"They haven't been so far. It's such a safe set-up, they have no reason to."

"But it would be too risky to do anything in the daylight. They might see you."

"That's why I'll wait until dark. With luck, it will all be over by morning."

"That's leaves us this afternoon, unless you have some-thing planned?"

She put her arm out and gently stroked the side of my face.

Rebecca had that way of making light of a bad situation, taking my mind off any of the danger which might be in-volved, clearing my thoughts and leaving me only with her. I succumbed willingly.

Somehow, we made our way to the bed, our clothes scat-tered throughout the dining room and hall as our emotions got the better of us, and by the time we reached the bed, we were both naked, falling heavily onto the soft padded quilt and connecting immediately. It was as if we were made for each other. Everything about Rebecca felt right—warm and welcoming. Inviting me to stay and enjoy the fruits of her body while mine yielded to every movement and touch she placed upon it.

Together we romped, wrestled, our bodies racked and quivered with each tremor that shook between us, never wanting to be released from this hold we had on each other. She was the wanton woman, licentious, her passions boiling over, unable to be tamed, while I, though the hunter, could not compete against such overwhelming voracity.

The end catapulted us both into that dreamlike state of erotic exhaustion, our bodies limp, weak, yet satisfied and I knew after a rest that we would both seek yet another round of animalistic lust.

Had it not been for the clock chiming three and awakening us to the time, we might have carried on until dark or further, but Rebecca's motherly instincts kicked in and she called an unhappy halt to our gluttonous behaviour as the children would not be that far away and had to be collected, while I needed time to prepare what I was about to do that night.

The solution had come to me in the flash, when our bodies were about to be engulfed in that combustible moment when bodies explode together, our minds ablaze with that fiery sensation which racks you to the core. Although not a vision, the flames that licked our bodies were symbolic of what was to come, a way of destroying what the men had come for, hopefully driving them out and getting rid of them, once and for all. Fire!

CHAPTER SEVENTEEN

I excused myself from the dinner table early before the children were sent to bed, returning to the barn to prepare for the night. There was no sign of fire in the sky now, but by midnight, I expected to see much of the forest on the opposite side of the creek ablaze. I dressed again, taking the black balaclava and wearing it on my head like a hat while I filled two empty drums with diesel from a fuel drum used for the tractor. I slipped the box of matches under the balaclava, and with the browning under my skivvy, I took the M16 off the bike and started off.

It was a good night for a fire — cool, but not chilly, with no sign of rain. I knew that where the crop was planted, there were plenty of dead leaves and branches — perfect fuel for a blaze. I made my way along the banks of the creek, taking note of the quiet camp situated on the opposite bank when I reached there. There was no guard, and I could make out the vehicles parked together and what looked like people sleeping beneath them and one near the fire which was starting to die down.

All was quiet in the area when I reached the shed and looked across the creek to the darkened forest area. I slipped into the water at a place I considered not too deep, wading out as far as possible, the water reaching my waist before levelling out. I held the rifle and the drums above the water line as I steadily made my way across until I reached solid ground. I moved quickly, scampering from the water into the shadows of the trees and through the cleared area of plants and into the mix of plants and foliage, starting to sprinkle the contents of the drums over everything as I made my way deeper into what was left of the crop.

Little time was wasted emptying the drums of fuel and, when done, I took the matches and struck one, dropping it onto the ground. In an instant, a fiery stream of flame spread throughout the crop, lighting the foliage and leaping up, the fire jumping from shrubs to plants and higher. It was drier than I'd thought and spread rapidly, reaching up into the trees, the branches and leaves of the eucalypt trees combusting and crackling loudly. It was no place to be, the fire spreading its tentacles in all directions. I ran wildly through the bush to escape, but in the darkness and my haste, I didn't see the trip wire that was laid across the ground.

My foot connected with the wire, tripping me headlong into the scrub. Instant images flashed through my mind as I waited for some explosion, but it never happened. Instead, an alarm sounded, a shrieking noise barely audible above the noise now being created by the roaring fire. I got to my feet, cursing Tex, as he must have been responsible since the wire wasn't there the first time I visited the crop — nothing was. Although there was some distance between the crop and the camp, I guessed that by now they would have heard the alarm and if not, the crackling of the fire and possible glowing of the flames.

"Shit!" I limped, feeling the pain in my ankle as I started off. I had a long way to go to circumvent the fire and cross to the far side of the creek. "Why that leg?" I whined, thinking of the months of recuperating I'd done after the operation on it to remove the bullets and fragments. There was no choice but to keep going — drive myself through the pain, something I knew a little about. I heard what sounded like a motor and men shouting as I made my way through the trees before turning and heading towards the creek. By the time I reached the water, the fire had taken a vicious hold and was moving through the forest and undergrowth towards the camp, making it impossible for the men to fight with limited equipment.

Making my way into the water, I swam and paddled my way across to the far side, looking back at the destruction the fire was causing, the flames licking at some of the tallest of trees. I crawled onto the bank and sat for a moment watching, letting the cool water take the heat from my throbbing ankle. It wasn't broken, I was sure, just badly sprained or twisted, but what a time for that to happen with a couple of miles to trudge through the dark to get back to the barn. Moving away from the water, I made my way back, keeping an eye on the opposite bank where the fire appeared to be burning to the waterline, the reflection of the flames dancing over the water.

The camp was in turmoil. The cattle they had rounded up that afternoon were being released and racing madly for safety while the men were trying to put their horses in the trailer and prepare to leave. I smiled, thinking it was a job well done until I heard the whirring of bullets overhead and around me. I dived for cover, unsure where they came from, but the one that hit a few feet from me indicated the shooter had me in his sights. I could make out the activity going on, but without a night scope to get a more accurate picture, a shot would be difficult.

It was as difficult to crawl as it was to walk, but I had no wish to stay in one place and become a sitting target for Tex. If he did have a night scope, his sights were well off target, or perhaps he was just shooting blind and hoping to snare a kill. At the distance and with the confusion, the shot would be difficult with the rifle I'd seen him with, but I knew not to underestimate him and wasn't sure what other firearms he had in the cabin of the truck. The bullets stopped coming and I lifted my head and looked across the creek. The two vehicles made a hurried exit from the camp as the fire appeared to jump from treetop to treetop, igniting the trees as it moved. I partly stood, anxious to see if the bullets might start again, but nothing.

Without a crutch, it was difficult to walk, but somehow, I managed to struggle, finally making my way back to the dam, with only the long haul up the hill to go. There was no sign of the trucks, so I guessed they had gone. Got away clean. I couldn't care less, so long as Rebecca was safe and that was the end of this. I looked up the hill thinking how easy it would be if I had the bike, but that wasn't to be, so I started off hobbling up the incline.

I'd barely reached halfway when the first hail of bullets whistled past me. I dropped to the ground thinking that all the men had gone. There was nothing left here for them, so why were they still here? Or was it only Tex? I pushed myself forward up the hill waiting for the next shot, hoping that the darkness would give me enough protection until I reached the barn. A bullet ploughed into the ground only a metre away and I rolled, hoping to see where my adversary was. Another two shots in quick succession hit the ground and I saw the flash of the gun in the darkness. I raised the M16 and fired a number of shots into the darkness, then rolled again, pushing myself upwards towards the top of the hill.

Again, the bullets sprayed into the ground around me and I wondered if he was playing with me. Whatever, I was not interested in being used for a clay pigeon shoot and badly needed to find some protection, which meant I had to reach the barn and safety. As it was, I'd only brought the one magazine for the gun and knew after a few more bursts that would be gone. Bullets danced around me again and I instinctively returned the fire, standing and attempting to run the last few metres to the barn, which turned out to be more of hop and jump as I scrambled for the open door.

Burning pain in my leg caused me to buckle and drop, then

crawl. I knew I had been hit in the same leg the VC had so badly damaged. I groaned and struggled towards the hay bales where I'd hidden the other gun and ammunition. I sat up and checked the leg, which was bleeding profusely. I took the belt from my pants and tightened it about my thigh, hoping that might stem the flow of blood. I placed the browning on a bale within reach and searched in the dark of the corner, found the gun, then quickly brushed it down and checked it. I pulled out from between the bales a number of clips, placing them beside me. I waited. I had a perfect view of whoever made an entry through the rear door.

My thoughts drifted to that final day of my war in Vietnam and the patrol we were sent out on. Nineteen of us in a mop-up operation, searching for stragglers after there had been an attack on a village not far from the base. Command had told us it was unlikely we'd find anything, but to be sure, they needed a reconnaissance of the area.

As sometimes happens, they got it totally wrong! An hour out and in the middle of a thickly wooded jungle-draped area in miserable weather, the enemy was waiting, watching as we walked unknowingly into their ambush. Sniper fire rang out from above, and somewhere in the shadows and we all instinctively dropped to the ground searching for cover. A call from our platoon leader, Lieutenant Sharp, throwing orders and calling for casualties was answered with shouts, bringing more shots and returning gunfire. Then silence. I looked around slowly, watching for movement, but there was nothing I could see. The rain was as much an enemy as those we couldn't see. Water running into our eyes and turning the ground to mud. Wylie, our signal man, was lying prone on the ground not far from me. I whispered to him, unsure if he was hit or not. There was no response.

I wasn't sure where Conner or Wayne was. One had taken point while the other was in the line, and we were strung out, unprepared.

I whispered again to Wylie, urging him to find protective cover, with no results. Sporadic bursts of gunfire rang out with our leader again calling out about causalities. Bullets clipped the tree I'd found cover behind, sending splinters of wood spraying through the air. I ducked my head, sinking into the soft wet earth. A call went out to signal back to base, but I knew Wylie wasn't responding. I called him again, but nothing. Someone had to get word back to base, or the consequences would be dire. I had reasonable cover, so crouched low and dashed and dived to where Wylie was lying and fell heavily to the ground, against him, muddy water and blood splashing over me – I waited. I nudged him. Nothing. The blood ponding on the wet ground coming from a head wound made me realize there was nothing I could do.

I reached for the radio and started to send a message, keeping low, when a number of shots rang out again. I felt the dull thump as they hit Wylie's lifeless body and gave a quick assessment of the situation and our position to base in case one of the shots hit the radio and we were left with no communications. Again, the lieutenant called out, this time yelling for Wylie to get out a message, bringing more heated gunfire. From somewhere a grenade was thrown, hitting the earth and showering the area with mud and vegetation. Message sent, I saw my chance and raced back to the protection of the trees where I'd been, but not quickly enough. The single gunfire turned suddenly to machine gun fire and ripped a path along the ground and caught my leg as I dived for cover. It was turning out to be not one of my better days!

I wasn't sure how many times I'd been hit, but I couldn't feel my leg and the blood was running freely. Bullets pounded into the tree I was behind as I buried myself in the slushy ground. Then all hell broke loose with machine gun and small arms fire coming from all directions. The ground was broken by the explosion of grenades as they blasted nearby, showering the area with more mud and splinters of wood. I heard one of our men cry out and return fire, but there was nothing to see. The best I could do was spray the area with bullets and hope I hit something.

As the shooting lulled, I took the strap from the butt of the gun and wound it tightly around my thigh. There was blood on the ground and my pants leg was soaked, and my leg felt a dead weight to try to move. Grenades exploded not far from me and I heard men scream and yell out in a foreign tongue, so I knew I was not alone and some of my group was still active – thank heavens. I only hoped they didn't delay back at the base in sending help, because I wasn't sure how many of us were left, or how long we might even survive. Small arms fire sounded out again and I heard the chatter of the M60 machine gun as it returned fire. I moved to one side to get a view ahead of me, but the enemy was too well concealed. I pointed my gun and fired blindly into the shadows, spraying the area until the clip emptied, at least showing there remained some resistance in the patrol.

The quiet was the worst. Your ears played tricks on you, picking up every small sound, every movement. My sight was becoming a blur, the rain still falling and I felt myself weakening, barely able to replace the clip and move the rifle into position for another shot. More gunfire rang out and the ground around me spurted mud and undergrowth as the bullets skipped by me. I returned fire, shooting blindly, my ears picking up sounds of motors, but my eyes failing to see. There was a sting in my shoulder and then darkness . . .

When I heard the noise, I was unsure where it came from. I had a perfect vision of the rear opening of the barn, but not of the front. If it was Tex, he was making the clumsiest entry, bumping and knocking things in the dark. Then I suddenly had a vision of Rebecca wandering about in the dark looking for me and thought it could have been her.

"Who is it?" I shouted out, revealing my presence and whereabouts.

"Is that you, Richard?" a gruff voice answered.

"Daley? What the hell are you doing here?" I asked, struggling to stand to see where he was.

"I had a report the house was on fire out here. It's about the only bloody thing that's not. What the bloody hell have you been doing?"

He made his way to near where I was leaning against the bales.

"Are you all right?" he asked when he saw me, unsure what was happening.

"Yes, at present, but you better get down. I'm expecting company." I let my body slide down the bales until I was back on the ground.

He crouched down beside me seeing the M16 and the handgun I had on the bale. "What sort of company?"

"The sort with blond hair and beady eyes and a lethal aim. I'm sure you'd have a wanted poster on him." I gasped, the pain in my leg becoming unbearable.

"You need some help, mate. I'll give you a hand and get you over to the house."

He started to get up, putting his arms about me to lift me up.

"No. We can't take this there and endanger Rebecca and the kids. Whatever happens, we'll have to play it out here," I told him, letting him lower me back to the ground.

"I'll go for help. There are extra men down near the gate. A Constable and a few firefighters."

"And a killer on the loose up here. Take the Browning, but keep under cover. I'm not sure what he's using, but when he wants to be, he can be downright dangerous." I chuckled through the pain.

He reached over and picked up the gun and started to stand when a shot rang out, the bullet hitting him in the shoulder. He dropped the gun and himself to the ground beside me and yelped in pain. "Fucking shit-head. Doesn't he know I'm the law?"

"I don't think he cares who the hell you are. It's me he's after."

"That's no bloody excuse to shoot me," he cried, grimacing

in pain and holding his shoulder, blood flowing from the wound. "What the hell did you do to piss him off?"

"If you've got an hour or two, I'll tell you, or would you like the shorter version?"

"Cut to the chase. What the hell did you do?"

"The Major and his mate have been growing marijuana on the property and shipping it overseas to the war zone. I stumbled on it recently and since then, there's been bad blood between us."

"And Rebecca?"

"She didn't know a thing about it until I told her."

"And this character?" he asked referring to the gunman.

"Tex works for Charlie, the Major's partner. He's sort of a tidy-up man. They don't like any loose ends."

"And you're a loose end?"

"Pain in the arse would be a better word. How are you holding up?"

He chuckled. "We're a great pair — you with your leg and me with the shoulder. What's he waiting for?"

"He strikes me as the type who enjoys his work. He's probably hoping we'll both bleed to death. You know . . . slow and agonising."

"Fuck him. I'm going to make a break for it. Can you cover me?" He gasped, clutching his shoulder while starting to lift himself up at the same time.

"I can, but where the hell is he?" I asked unsure where the last shot came from.

Another shot rang out and hit the bales above Daley's head, stopping his movement and forcing him back. "That was short lived. Did you see where the shot came from?"

"Over there . . . to the left," I indicated.

"Another half hour and it will be coming light. If the boys hear the shots, they might come running to investigate. Can you return fire?" he asked, groaning as the pain in his shoulder became worse.

Tonight was the only time I fired a gun since that fateful day, and on that occasion, I was fighting for my life and those around me, much the same as I was now. I sent a spray of bullets in the direction of the shot, blindly hoping Tex might be in the path of one. Then waited. There was no response — not that I'd expected one. He'd probably moved, knowing we were both casualties and he had us pinned down.

"Do you think if I talked to this shit-head, he'd listen?" Daley asked.

"Why don't you let me? You don't look like you could talk your way out of a wet paper bag at present." I looked at him holding his shoulder and the blood soaking his once clean uniform.

"I'm the law," he responded as though that would mean anything.

"Tex!" I shouted. "There's a copper here that you've badly wounded. Let him go and I'll throw out my guns."

There was silence, though I doubted Tex would respond as he had the upper hand. I was wrong. A grenade came bouncing in from outside rolling along the ground towards us.

"Oh shit!" I saw Daley's eyes widen as he waited for the blast, but then it spewed smoke throughout the building making it impossible to see a few feet in front of your face. Daley gave me a quick and uncomfortable glance. "What is it?"

"Smoke grenade. He's on the move." I fired the M16 into the pall of smoke, spreading the bullets from outside to inside unsure what I was hitting, before hearing the click as the clip ran out. I grabbed for another clip, but before I could load, I had the nozzle of a rifle poked into my face.

CHAPTER EIGHTEEN

As the smoke started to clear, I looked along the barrel and saw the grinning face of Tex, staring down at me.

"Is this the son-of-a-bitch that shot me?" Daley asked, unable to do anything more than give him a *you're under arrest* look, which meant nothing to Tex.

"You *would* interfere, copper. This was between me and him," Tex said, sneering at Daley.

"You know what the penalty is for shooting a police officer?" Daley asked as if that would worry Tex.

"I'm shaking." Tex smiled. "And you, soldier boy, on your feet. I'm going to give you a chance to escape." He poked the rifle into my chest. "You've made a mess of this operation, and I'm going to make a mess of you."

"You can't shoot him in cold blood. He can barely walk," Daley protested as I struggled to my feet, the guns out of reach of both of us.

"I wouldn't be worried about him, copper. After I'm finished with him, I'm coming back for you." He grinned and shoved the butt of the rifle into the wounded shoulder of Daley causing him to scream out and swear in agony.

I was unsteady on my feet. In fact, I could barely feel my leg, which felt like lead. "Why don't you just shoot me and put me out of my misery," I spat out, feeling nothing but contempt for the man.

"My boss wants you dead and you will be, but I want you to suffer. Do you know how much you've cost him?" He shook his head. "You had every opportunity to get out. What was it, an attack of the morals, or has it got something to do with the woman?"

I replied bitterly, "Neither. I lost some good mates up there. We were fighting for what we believed was the right thing, but then your boss and his mates turn the war into a fiasco by selling drugs and making themselves rich at the expense of the boys trying to do what's right. Bastards that make money out of a miserable situation. I guess I'd had enough,"

"Pity . . . he could have used a chap like you if you'd have accepted his offer."

"I wasn't that desperate."

"Too bad. Take a hike." He prodded me with the barrel of the gun

I looked at him. I was barely able to stand, let alone walk away from him. "Why don't you just shoot us both and get it over with?" I looked over at Daley and saw he was unconscious, or looked that way, and I could only think *lucky bastard*. I watched as Tex lifted the rifle, pointing it in my direction. Whether my leg gave way or I instinctively fell I couldn't remember, but as I hit the ground, I heard the crack of the gun and rolled my way partly down the hill. Either the pain in my leg caused me to black out or I was dead—only the future would reveal the truth. *If I had a future?*

I awoke, strapped to a stretcher in the back of a vehicle with what appeared to be a male nurse sitting between me and Daley, who was lying opposite on another stretcher.

"Are we dead?" I asked the nurse, uncertain where we were or what had happened.

"Not by my calculations, but I'm not a doctor," he answered, a grin on his face.

"Where are we?"

"Back of an ambulance, waiting to take you both to hospital. Seems the pair of you are bloody lucky to still be here."

He wasn't a great help, but at least I found out we had both survived — but what the hell happened?

"And him?" I indicated Daley, who appeared unconscious.

"He'll be fine. He's had a dose of morphine to ease the pain. He'll sleep for a while." He told me I had the same, but mine hadn't kicked in — or had it? I was feeling no pain.

"What happened?" I asked again.

"I'm not sure, but there's a Constable running around who might know. Do you want me to find him?"

I shook my head. "No. I'm sure they'll be talking with us before much longer. Will it be long before we leave?" I started feeling slightly dopey.

"A couple of minutes. Apparently, there's a lot to clean up."

I wasn't sure what he meant by that, but the morphine he gave me was starting to kick in, bringing back that darkness of old I'd long been trying to forget.

When I next woke, I was in a small ward in hospital, my leg bound in bandage and splints and held in a sling, making me bed-bound. Beside me in the next bed, Sergeant Daley was sleeping peacefully, his arm and shoulder bandaged and in a tight sling. Tubes ran from saline and blood bags to our arms while machines buzzed and clicked beside us both. I wondered if I'd have to go through the same rehabilitation program I went through last time, or even have a permanent limp–at least the leg was still attached to my body.

It was much the same feeling waking up in the 1st field hospital at Vung Tau. Tubes running here and there and blood slowly replacing what I'd lost and no idea what had happened. It took two days before I was finally told the story, and that was from Conner, who had survived the ordeal with only a shrapnel wound to the arm and was being treated in another ward. Apparently, we had walked into an ambush by the VC. Not just a few stragglers as we'd been led to believe, but quite a large force.

We were well on the receiving end until the relief force arrived with APC's and choppers to bring out the wounded. We lost five of the group in that action, Wylie and Wayne amongst them and another four on the serious list including myself. Enemy causalities were believed to be heavy, but as with most skirmishes the VC took their dead and wounded with them when they departed. I was the lucky one of the group being sent home, my fighting days over, and my days of attempting to walk again some weeks into the future. Conner was returning to the base, but we made arrangements that we'd meet up again on his return home.

That meeting was cancelled when I learned some months later he had been killed in another operation, not unlike the one we'd been through. It seemed like I went from one disaster to another at that time in my life, but it was a time I would never forget and it was etched in my memory until my dying day.

Curiosity was getting the better of me. I had no idea how long I'd been here and no recollection about what had happened. Tex would never have missed at that close range, so something had happened to deny him his kill. And Daley was here with me. Tex had promised Daley would be next, though I didn't need his company wherever I was going, but the whole business mystified me. When he finally woke, he was as baffled as me, having blacked out after being hit with the rifle butt by Tex. A doctor visited both of us checking how we were feeling, but he was as vague about what happened as our memories of the incident.

A day after we woke in the hospital beds, Daley's sidekick, a Constable Molloy, paid us both a visit. By now, Daley was sitting up and even allowed out of bed, while I still had my leg raised and held in the sling, but we were both fully conscious and busting for answers.

"Okay," Molloy said sitting down on a chair between the beds. "I need you both to fill in the blanks as to what happened. Can I start with you, Mr. Scott? I believe you were helping out Mrs. Greenshaw, doing odd jobs about the farm?"

"Molloy. I know all that. Get to the point, what happened at the end? That psycho killer idiot?" Daley asked.

It was obvious Daley did not want to hear my life story over again.

"What happened to Tex?"

"That was Mrs. Greenshaw's doing. She shot him. I've spoken to her and got a statement, but it appears to be self-defence. She mentioned he was going to kill you both."

"Rebecca . . ." I murmured aloud, stunned that she was even there, let alone saved our lives.

"She speaks very highly of you," Molloy said, thinking nothing about it.

"She *thinks* very highly of you," Daley mimicked, giving me a cheesy grin.

"It sounds like I owe her my life. Is she all right?" I could barely believe it. "She wasn't hurt at all?"

"A bit shook up, but that's only natural after what she did."

"We've both got a lot to thank her for," Daley commented. "What else have you got, Constable?"

"It's been busy." Molloy grinned. "I should be up for promotion after all this."

"Stop fantasizing with yourself and get on with it," Daley said, which sounded more like a growl.

"With the help from Mrs. Greenshaw and the aid from a couple of firefighters, we were able to stop a truck after it had broken through the fencing of the property and attempted to escape along the northbound roadway. We've been able to seize a truckload of marijuana bound for a cattle property many miles from here, where a large consignment of the drug was found and confiscated. The owner of the property escaped by means of a light plane but was arrested with another man sometime later. It appears the group was sending drugs overseas to the military. The military says they will investigate and take any further action that is necessary," Molloy concluded. "You might get more out of them, but for me, it was like talking to a wall."

I wasn't sure if the Constable looked up expecting accolades from us both, but when nothing happened, he continued.

"Also, three men were detained driving a large cattle truck and towing a horse float, which was also believed to be part of the group. One man was taken to hospital with severe lacerations, but is expected to make a full recovery."

"That'll be Ray. He's not a bad type, and if you treat him right, he'll sing like a canary," I told Molloy. "Tex was responsible, cutting him up when I'd convinced him to leave, hoping to split their forces. It didn't work, unfortunately."

"Regardless, I believe we got them all," the Constable said with a smile.

"And the Major?" Daley asked, not having heard mention of him.

"Major?"

"Major John Greenshaw, retired. Has he been arrested?" Daley gritted the words between his teeth.

Molloy looked down at his paperwork. "He was the partner of one Colonel Charles Field, retired. They've both been arrested attempting to flee the country, illegally, by small plane. The police are investigating further, going through their property and papers."

"Good. That gives me some satisfaction. How about you?" Daley asked looking over at me.

"They can lock him up and throw away the key," I replied. "How will Rebecca fair in all this?"

"How do you mean?" Molloy asked.

"The drugs were grown on her property," I said, not wanting to make a big thing of it.

"Without her knowledge," Daley added, helping me out.

"There were no drugs found on Mrs. Greenshaw's property," Molloy answered. "A lot of the property on the north side of the creek has been burned out by the fire. We did find quite a few head of cattle running loose, but they've been contained."

"So, she's in the clear, Scott. What are you going to do about it?" Daley asked, more as an inquisitive friend, than a copper.

"How do you mean? She's a married woman, with kids."

"She's an *unhappily* married woman with two adorable kids. Since you've been out there, I've never seen her so happy, and the kids have taken a liking to you," Daley said making small talk.

"How do you know that?"

"I've spoken to her a few times recently, and her kids go to school with mine. Kids talk, and most of what they say is truthful. It's only when they get older that they start telling lies and trying to put things over you." He chuckled to himself.

"So, I need a statement from you, Mr. Scott and I'll need one from you also, Sarge," Molloy said trying to sound officious.

"That's Sergeant Daley to you, Molloy. And that can wait. Can't you see the chap's in pain here? I'll be out in a couple of days, I'll help you get your mess sorted out then," he told Molloy, bringing an end to the interview.

Molloy packed up what he'd brought and left, leaving us lying on our beds.

"Your wife hasn't been to see you yet," I said to Daley.

"It's been *no visitors* up till now, but I think that will be relaxed after today. Besides, I'm getting out in a couple of days, but I guess you'll be here for a bit longer."

"Seems like a lifetime," I replied looking at my leg.

That afternoon, I met Daley's wife, Jo, which I guessed was short for Joanna, who came to visit. I was hoping Rebecca might have had the time to come and see me, but that wasn't to be. But it did give me more time to get to know Daley, and I found he was not unlike the boys I'd known in the service. Strange, when you get to know some coppers, you find they're not that different from some of your mates.

Two days later, Daley was discharged, leaving me alone in the ward, checked once a day by the doctor and visited occasionally by the nurse, although I only had to ring the bell and she was there. Rebecca still hadn't visited, and I was sure there was something wrong. Molloy had said she wasn't hurt, but I was beginning to doubt that. Something had to be wrong. I had that feeling of déjà vu, not unlike I'd experienced once before, though this was totally different.

By the time I arrived back in Australia I was moving slowly about on crutches – though painfully.

Most of my day was spent lying about on the hospital bed waiting for visitors who never came. I had written to Eleanor and informed her about what had happened and where I was, but had had no reply, and it wasn't until I was released from hospital some two months later and allowed home that I found out the reason why. Home was no longer home, and Eleanor was no longer there. I found out after speaking with people that knew her that she'd left town with my best mate, taking with her all our savings after selling off most of my equipment from the building business, which was now defunct.

I was shattered, broke and very disillusioned, scraping up enough money to buy a cheap secondhand motorbike and determined to make a new start, somewhere, anywhere as long as it was well away from there. I returned back and forth to hospital until the therapy was finished and I was given the all clear, then set out, determined to never again be duped by some female who supposedly loved me and had my best interests at heart. It was a learning curve some males probably go through when they're smitten by the weaker sex.

I kicked myself . . . Time to grow up!

The next day after the doctor had been around to visit, the nurse came in with a smirk on her face. "You have a visitor. Do you feel like company?"

"Who?" I asked stupidly, as I only knew Rebecca and now Jo and I could see no reason for Jo to be calling on me. The nurse made sure the bed was respectable and checked that everything was in place as it should be.

"A lady." She winked and grinned. "She's a bit nervous, but I told her not to be. I won't disturb you, but if you do need anything just ring the bell," she told me as she left the room closing the door.

I waited.

It seemed like an eternity, watching for the door to move and nothing was happening. Finally, the door slowly opened and Rebecca stepped in looking around the room and smiling to me as she closed the door. She came slowly towards the bed. I smiled and reached out to take her hand. She looked at me and then the leg. "The nurse said they put pins and plates in. Does it hurt?"

"Not really. They still have me doped up a bit. How are you? I heard what happened. I was worried about you," I said trying to pull her closer.

"It's been traumatic. I wasn't sure how badly you were hurt, but Tom visited with me yesterday and we had a talk. I felt a lot better, but it was . . ." She dropped suddenly onto the bed beside me, her face against mine and the tears starting to run down her cheeks. "I thought I'd lost you. I was so scared." She sobbed.

"You were wonderful. You saved both Tom and me. Tex was going to kill us."

"I know. I heard." She held me tightly hugging me,

sobbing gently.

"Do you want to talk about it?" I whispered. I put my arm around her, my hand gently caressing her back.

She lifted her head and nodded. "Tom wanted to know as well. I don't think I'll ever forget it."

"It might get easier over time," I said trying to ease her pain, but knowing the pain never goes.

"I heard shots and got up and went out to the verandah and saw the forest was ablaze. I heard more shots that I thought were coming from in the barn and went back inside and got into my dressing gown and took the gun from the drawer. You said you thought it worked, but I'd never fired one before. I crept over to the barn and heard that man talking to you. It was dark and smoky and I thought at first the barn was on fire, but no flames. I crept closer and saw him lift you up, and then he hit Tom. I took the gun with two hands and held it up, pointing it at him. I balked. My finger had trouble squeezing the trigger, but when I saw him push you out and bring up his gun, I fired. I don't know how many times I fired, but the gun went click in the end." She gave a half-hearted smile. "I must have hit him, because when I opened my eyes, he was lying on the ground."

She kissed and hugged me again.

"I was so scared I'd lost you."

I held her close. "You're never going to lose me. I love you, Rebecca." It was how I felt, and I'd wished I'd said it when we were together before — when I could show her how much.

She lifted her head again, trying to stop sobbing, the mascara leaving dark streaks down her cheeks. "I love you, too." She grinned. "You do know I'm a married woman?"

"With two kids," I added. "But if you and the kids will have an old crippled man to help out around the place, I'd be willing to apply for the position."

"Any position?" She queried, that sexy smile I was so used

158

to seeing, returning. "Do you have a preference?"

"Trust you."

"What are we going to do about Geoffrey?" The smile faded.

"There's not a lot either of us can do at present." I looked down at my leg. "I might send him a letter and charge him for the time I've lost, owing to his business partners, or maybe tell him I'll take his wife in lieu of wages."

She looked astounded at the suggestion. "You wouldn't, would you?"

"I'll need some recompense for all the time I have to stay here . . . alone . . . without you to keep me warm. It seems only fair." I took the sympathetic approach.

She snuggled closer and whispered, "I can't give you all the recompense you deserve, but I can fulfil some of what you want."

I was pleased with that.

Rebecca spent the rest of the day lying with me and at times taunting me so badly that I worried the machines that were hooked up to me might sound off some alarm and bring a flood of medical staff into the room — most embarrassing!

CHAPTER NINETEEN

Within a few days, my leg was released from the sling and I was unhooked from the machines and tubes that had been my constant companion since I arrived at the hospital. Rebecca had been in every day after breaking the ice and finding I was not as badly damaged as she imagined I was, giving me something to look forward to. Each day, I grew stronger and I was finally allowed from the bed, with the aid of crutches which had been a familiar part of my life after returning from Vietnam.

It was the day before I was to be released into Rebecca's care that she came solemnly into the room, a look of anguish on her face. I was sitting on the edge of the bed after the physio had been, my leg healing well, but bearing the scars of two conflicts now. "Why the long face?" I asked, unsure what had happened.

"I received a telegram late yesterday," she answered opening her purse and taking out the envelope and passing it to me. I looked at her enquiringly, seeing it was addressed to her. "Open it."

I was possibly as hesitant as she had been in opening it, knowing what a telegram from the Defence Department could mean. It was simple and to the point.

It is with regret, we have to inform you, your husband Captain Geoffrey Greenshaw was shot down and killed while flying over enemy territory. Further information will be made available upon your request . . . when available. Condolences, etc, etc . . .

I looked up at Rebecca, whose eyes had welled up and appeared to be ready to burst into tears. "I'm sorry. I didn't know him, but . . ." I was trying to find the words.

"Don't be." She sniffled and wiped her nose.

"But . . . I know how you feel."

"Do you? The tears are not for him. They're for us. You do know what this means? We can be together . . . get married . . . if that's what you want?" She stooped down and kissed me. It seemed finally something was going right for the pair of us.

The following day, I was released from hospital in what could only be termed a carnival atmosphere. Most of the hospital staff was there, including my physio, along with what seemed to be most of the town that had turned out to get a glimpse of me, as I was wheeled out to the police car by Rebecca, where Tom and his wife Jo were waiting to drive us out to the farm. I felt extremely honoured, yet embarrassed to be treated this way after my initial contact with some of these people.

Angus smiled and waved to me as though we were old mates, and Rebecca pointed out Freddy the school bus driver, who we had held up just the one time when our lovemaking had got out of hand and all time had been forgotten. It was much the same with most people there. I had never met them, but they all regarded me as their friend and welcomed me into the community. Whether it was because of my stand against the drugs, or my love-affair with Rebecca, or my association with Tom that could have ended so untimely for us both, I wasn't sure, but it was inspiring and flattering to know I had so many people who seemed genuinely concerned for my wellbeing.

After briefly speaking with a few, Tom drove the car from the grounds and headed along the road to Rebecca's farm. "I doubt you'll be doing too much for the next few weeks?" Tom asked as he drove.

"I've got to come in for physio a couple of times a week, but it will be mainly rest until the leg is better," I replied.

"Rebecca asked Angus about crops and what he thought you should be planting out there."

"He was going to think about it and let me know," Rebecca answered, her head on my shoulder.

"He suggested you plant avocados and custard apples. They'll grow just about anywhere and as yet, they're not a widely popular commodity, but over time . . ." Tom told them.

"What would the cost be?" I asked, unsure how much Rebecca might have to spend on such a venture after all that had happened.

"Minimal. Angus can get some grafted trees at a good rate."

Tom turned and looked over at Rebecca and me in the back.

"I told him to get a couple of hundred for starters. That should give you something to do."

I sat up looking over at him. "You did *what*? I'm not sure I'm up to planting a heap of trees at present."

"That's fine. When they arrive, a group of us from town are coming out to do the planting. You'll just have to do the watering. Think you can manage that?" He grinned.

Rebecca spoke up. "Tom, I'm not sure I can afford that at present."

"You don't have to. It's a starter present for the pair of you from the town's folk. Their way of saying *thanks*. You deserve it."

He stopped the car, and Jo got out to open the gate, then waited as he drove through to close it. "In a few years, you should have a yearly crop and become self-producing after that." He drove on through the water and up the hill to the homestead and stopped the car a few feet from the steps to the verandah.

"It would have been easier if you'd driven to the barn," I told him looking at how far I had to walk.

"Rebecca told me you were staying in the house," he said, turning around to face me.

I looked at Rebecca, slightly stunned.

"Tom and Jo know our situation. I spoke with the children, and they'd like to have you stay in the house with us and I'd like to have a man about again as well, so you'll be staying in my room," she said with a smile.

"Are you sure . . . the children?"

"They're both happy about the idea. You're going to need care and attention for the next few weeks, and I can't be running back and forth to the barn so this is the best alternative. I really didn't think you'd mind," she explained.

"This is the country, Richard," Jo said, breaking her silence. "We're not like city folk out here. We don't talk behind people's backs. We do know what goes on at times, and we do know right from wrong, and it wouldn't be right for two people who love each other to be living so far apart and under such difficult circumstances. I'm sure when your leg's healed, you'll do the right thing by Rebecca and the kids."

There was nothing in the way she said that to indicate anything more than what she said. It appeared she knew Rebecca well and had sized me up from what Tom had told her about me. And she was right. Once the leg was right again and I could work and do what was needed about the place, I would do the right thing by Rebecca. I had already made up my mind about that.

They helped me out, and Tom took hold of me and virtually carried me up the stairs and onto the verandah, where Rebecca was waiting with the crutches. It was obvious his shoulder had healed well. "Would you stay and have some tea with us?" she asked Tom and Jo.

Tom shook his head. "Not this time. You've got enough to do. When he's more mobile, we'll come out for dinner and bring the kids."

"I'll look forward to it," Rebecca said as we watched them get back in the car and drive out.

"He turned out to be all right," I said, watching the car drive out of sight.

"I told you he was. Now let's get you to bed," she said, prompting me to make my way around to the bedroom doors off the verandah.

"I'm not all that tired," I complained. "You do know that's all I've been doing for weeks now – lying about?"

"You don't have to tell me."

She helped me through to the bed and settled me down. "The kids won't mind me sleeping in the same bed their father used to sleep in?"

She looked around the room. "Where else are you going to sleep in here?"

"You know what I –"

"They know their father won't be home, ever. And they know I'm looking after you from now on. And when you're well enough, you'll be looking after all of us – forever."

"Are they happy about that?" I asked, worried it might be too much, too soon.

"Ask them when they get home." She snuggled close on the bed beside me. "Until then, though, I've got a lot to catch up on." She kissed me warmly.

I was sitting up in bed when Toby came through, standing at the door as though unsure he should enter or wait until Helen was with him to come closer. They both walked nervously to the side of the bed, looking at me and my leg as though I was someone to be feared. "How was school?" I asked, hoping to break the ice.

Toby nodded, while Helen looked closer at the bandaged leg. "Does it hurt?" she asked.

"Only when I walk on it," I answered.

"Are you going to be our new father?" Helen asked with the same directness as her mother, which left me floundering for a moment.

"Would that bother you both?"

"I'm not sure," Toby replied hesitantly.

"Would you get angry and shout at us?" Helen asked.

"What for?"

"Dad used to yell at us and smack us if we were naughty," Toby told me.

I had no answer to that. The children had always been well behaved when I was about, and I had no idea what fear had been instilled in them by their father, or grandfather, but it did have them both talking.

Luckily Rebecca entered the room and the children went quiet again, saving me the trouble of coming forward with an answer. "They're not annoying you at all?" she asked.

"No. We were just talking."

"I mentioned to Toby that when your leg was better you might take him to the dam and teach him to swim. I told him you were an excellent swimmer," Rebecca said.

"Could you?" Toby asked.

"Certainly. I can have you swimming in no time," I told him confidently.

"What about me?" Helen asked.

"You too. In fact, we can all go swimming there. Your mother included."

"That would be fun," Rebecca agreed, the children both happy with that news.

"I'm also a whiz at doing homework and can speak a little

Vietnamese, if anyone's interested," I offered.

"Don't get too enthusiastic, Richard. You've got plenty of time to impress the children." She looked over at Toby and Helen. "Now, I think you should let Richard rest. You don't want to wear him out."

"No. Leave that for your mother," I said jokingly, not that the children understood, although I did get a frown from Rebecca as she ushered the children out.

"I'll be back later with your dinner," she told me as they all left, returning the room to the quiet it had been.

After they left, my old mate came quietly skulking into the room, unsure what all the fuss was about. Red put his head up and gave a whimper to let me know he'd missed me over the past few weeks. I patted him kindly, and told him when things were better I'd take him for another ride on the bike, which more then satisfied him.

There's nothing like time in hospital or long periods of bed rest to allow a person to reflect, think back to the past and hypothesize about the future. Over the past few weeks, I'd had plenty of time for that. I had been lucky, though at times I doubted that. I was still alive and breathing, which was more than what I could say for my three wartime buddies. I heard that Conner copped it not long after returning to active duty — a land mine that had gone unnoticed had severed my last remaining link to my time in the conflict that had disrupted so many lives. I had all my limbs, though some were not as agile and unscathed as they were before the war, but over time, they would mend, perhaps leaving a limp in my gait.

My love life, which on my return was in tatters, had been the reason for my wanderings, and as much as I did not believe in fate, it must have been fate which had directed me here. My meeting with Rebecca by the roadside and my curiosity to help brought us together, along with all the dramas that ensued. But what would life be without dramas? I'd had enough in the past few years to last me a lifetime, but I knew there would be more along the way. I now felt confident that with Rebecca by my side, together we could meet and defeat any obstacle that lay in our path.

The ghosts of old mates would always be with me, but not haunting or tormenting as they had been. Instead, it would only be the good times that I would remember. The rest I would commit to the deepest, darkest corners of my mind and hopefully, in time, erase.

I now had a new life, someone that loved and cared for me as much as I for her. And children, something that had never entered my thoughts before, was now a reality. I smiled and lay back, my thoughts exhausting me. How fickle a life can be? A war without substance? A married woman with two children? And a lost soul searching for . . . Whatever, I knew I had found my life again, with Rebecca.

YOU MAY ALSO ENJOY THE FOLLOWING FROM EXTASY BOOKS INC:

Tempting Fate
B.D. Ward

Excerpt

The days dragged by with no word from Col. Janine had made sure the phone was handy so there was no way she could miss the call. Doubts clouded her mind. Had he just been playing her? He was good at that. Did he really want to help, or was he just saying that? Did he still bear a grudge about what happened all those years before?

Jason was being his usual fidgety self, reading the paper at one time before watching the television, then going and lying down before picking up a book and reading a few pages then becoming restless again. He'd been like that for weeks before and after the operation as though he had some foreboding of the results before they were announced. And when they were summoned back to the doctor's surgery for the results he acted as though he was prepared and fully expected what he was told, until they reached home when he broke down and sobbed for hours, cursing the doctors, life, his maker, and anyone else he could recall having been part of his existence. From that time on, he'd done nothing but mope about, whinge and complaining about the least little thing, asking anyone who would listen, why?

It was a side of him Janine had never seen, and wished she never had, and even though she dreaded the loss, their life had been a happy, full, and contented one. She had nothing to complain about, and for that matter, neither did Jason. They had two beautiful children, grown up now, with children of their own. That was life. You were born and you died, everyone knew that. It was purely a matter of when and how, and none of that was of our making. So we were led to believe. It was written in that Book of Life that is opened when we're born and closed upon our death. Everything that happens in between is recorded for that Higher Authority, and as Janine had told him, "It's useless worrying about what you have got up to in the past, since there is no way you'll ever be able to redeem yourself. But on a brighter note, there'll be a glut of people just like you waiting for that final assessment."

Oddly, she was coping well, although the worst was yet to come. Now in their fifties, they were well-off, owned their home and had a good sum of money in the bank, so she felt confident that without Jason, her life would still have some meaning. The idea of the surfing safari came to her after another of his mood swings in which he told her of the many things he'd wished he'd done, and she'd remembered it was one wish he'd held from the early days of their marriage. He regretted the fight and bust up of the group, and although he frequently saw Charlie, he was too proud or stubborn to pick up the phone and talk with Col. If only he had, it would have made life so much easier.

The phone rang, and before the second ring, she had the receiver to her ear. "Hello!"

"Janine?"

"Col?"

"It's on," was all he said.

For a moment, she remained quiet.

"Did you hear? I've organized it all."

"How? When?" she asked, her doubts evaporating as she listened.

"It was a bit difficult, but I tracked Blue down. The bastard lives in Bathurst now, and would you believe, he's still married to that bitch, Carol?"

"And he'll come, and go with you?"

"After a hell of a lot of plausible bullshit, which I laid out thick for Carol, but there is a condition."

She could hear Col draw a deep breath. "What?"

"She's coming too, but you'll have to put her up and look after her for the weekend. Is that alright?" he asked.

"I guess so. I haven't seen her for years. Has she changed much?"

"She sounded like the same bitchy person on the phone that I remember. At first, I thought she wanted to come with us to the beach, but then she told me she didn't give a stuff about what we got up to, so long as we brought him back in one piece. Not that he's much chop these days she reckons, but then all you women are the same."

"When is all this going to happen?" Janine asked.

"Not this weekend but the following. It's a long weekend so we'll be gone from Friday till Tuesday morning. Can you manage without him for that long?"

"It'll be hard, but I'll try," she replied, relieved.

"I've been wondering about a few things, though."

"What?" Janine asked, hearing doubt creep into Col's voice.

"Do you think he'll actually come when he knows I'm going to be there? I talked to Charlie and he's not sure. You might have to soften him up."

"I'll talk to him, but I was hoping to keep it a surprise."

"Tell him Friday morning, before we all arrive on your doorstep. That will surprise him." He laughed. "He's not on too much medication that he can't drink, is he?"

"He's got some, but I'm sure he'll keep himself in check," she told him.

"What about sex?"

Janine held herself back from laughing. "What have you got planned? I thought this was supposed to be a surfing weekend. You know, in the water with boards, not on the beach with broads?"

"It will be, but then, when we're out of the water, that's when we'll need the booze and broads." He laughed again. At least he hadn't lost his sense of humour. "Okay. Friday, late morning, we'll all be there. We're travelling light, so only the minimum of clothes. Is that understood? Think you can arrange all that?"

"I'm sure I can," she replied thankfully, unsure if he was serious about the broads.

"Good. We'll see you then," Col said and hung up, leaving her near to tears holding the phone.

"Who was that?" Jason asked, standing in the doorway watching her.

"Another charity asking for donations," she replied quickly.

"Been giving to cancer funds for forty years, and they still don't have a cure, but boy they have fancy offices and luxury cars. Makes me so bloody mad," he ranted, storming off.

"I hope this might be the cure you need," Janine said quietly under her breath.

About the Author

To say a little is never enough and too much is bragging, but never the less—

Born and schooled in Gympie, Queensland, but spent most of my working life on the Coast, building houses and units and running associated business for around thirty-five years. Married, with three grown-up children, who have in turn produced a number of beautiful grandchildren.

In my early years I was a keen sportsman, playing football, hockey, surfing and more, but now am quite content to watch. I enjoy most music and spent time in a number of rock bands in those early days.

I have settled into writing, although not comfortably at times—especially with cyber use, but after completing the *Ruhr* series of books, I have broadened my imagination to include *Search* and various upcoming titles. As in *Ruhr*, *Search* uses actual places and some historical facts, but the rest is storytelling, and I hope an enjoyable read.

www.ingramcontent.com/pod-product-compliance
Lightning Source LLC
Chambersburg PA
CBHW060819120626
46557CB00001B/287